That doesn't look like the Mr. Pruitt I know, Wishbone thought, looking in the classroom window.

Without a word of greeting, Mr. Pruitt opened a book and said, "Class, turn to page one hundred seventy-six of *The Great Poets.* Begin with the chapter on Robert Frost."

Most of the students looked confused. Sam said, "Uh . . . Mr. Pruitt, we already finished the chapter on Robert Frost."

Mr. Pruitt glanced down at his book, embarrassed. "Oh, so we did. Well, then, let's go to the poetry of Ogden Nash."

The students looked even more confused. Joe said, "Mr. Pruitt? I think we did Ogden Nash last week."

Mr. Pruitt closed his book. A look of anger crept into his eyes.

"Well, then," Mr. Pruitt said, in an irritated tone, "since the class is so well versed with every poet in this book, there will be an examination tomorrow. I suggest you all spend the remainder of this hour studying!"

The Adventures of WISHBONE™
titles in Large-Print Editions:

The Adventures of WISHBONE™

DR. JEKYLL and MR. DOG

by Nancy Butcher
Based on the teleplay by John Perry and Stephanie Simpson
Inspired by *Strange Case of Dr. Jekyll and Mr. Hyde*
by Robert Louis Stevenson

WISHBONE™ created by Rick Duffield

5/2000 Gumdrop Books

Gareth Stevens Publishing
MILWAUKEE

This book is a work of fiction. The characters, incidents, and dialogues are products of the author's imagination and are not to be construed as real. Any resemblance to actual events or persons, living or dead, is entirely coincidental.

For a free color catalog describing Gareth Stevens' list of high-quality books and multimedia programs, call 1-800-542-2595 (USA) or 1-800-461-9120 (Canada). Gareth Stevens Publishing's Fax: (414) 225-0377.

Library of Congress Cataloging-in-Publication Data

Butcher, Nancy.
    Dr. Jekyll and Mr. Dog / by Nancy Butcher; [interior illustrations by Jane McCreary].
        p. cm.
    Originally published: Allen, Texas; Big Red Chair Books, © 1998.
(The adventures of Wishbone; #14)
    Summary: When Joe's neighbor undergoes a change of personality after meeting the man of her dreams, Wishbone is reminded of the mysterious relationship between the kind,well-respected Dr. Jekyll and the evil Mr. Hyde.
    ISBN 0-8368-2592-6 (lib. bdg.)
    [1. Dogs—Fiction. 2. Horror stories.] I. McCreary, Jane, 1950- ill.
II. Stevenson, Robert Louis, 1850-1894. Dr. Jekyll and Mr. Hyde. III. Title.
IV. Adventures of Wishbone; #14.
PZ7.B9715Dr   2000
[Fic]—dc21   99-051791

This edition first published in 2000 by
Gareth Stevens Publishing
1555 North RiverCenter Drive, Suite 201
Milwaukee, Wisconsin 53212 USA

© 1998 Big Feats! Entertainment. First published by Big Red Chair Books™, a Division of Lyrick Publishing™, 300 E. Bethany Drive, Allen, Texas 75002.

Edited by Kevin Ryan
Copy edited by Jonathon Brodman
Cover design by Lyle Miller
Interior illustrations by Jane McCreary
Wishbone photograph by Carol Kaelson

WISHBONE, the **Wishbone** portrait, and the Big Feats! Entertainment logo are trademarks and service marks of Big Feats! Entertainment.

Printed in the United States of America

1 2 3 4 5 6 7 8 9 04 03 02 01 00

For Christopher,

who loves stories, too

FROM THE BIG RED CHAIR . . .

Oh . . . hi! Wishbone here. You caught me right in the middle of some of my favorite things—books. Let me welcome you to THE ADVENTURES OF WISHBONE. In each of these books, I have adventures with my friends in Oakdale and imagine myself as a character in one of the greatest stories of all time. This story takes place in early fall, when Joe is twelve and he and his friends are in the sixth grade—during the first season of my television show. In **DR. JEKYLL AND MR. DOG**, I imagine I'm John Utterson, from Robert Louis Stevenson's adventure story **STRANGE CASE OF DR. JEKYLL AND MR. HYDE**. It's a hair-raising story about mystery, dark secrets, and a scientific experiment gone wrong!

You're in for a real treat, so pull up a chair and a snack and sink your teeth into **DR. JEKYLL AND MR. DOG!**

CHAPTER ONE

Wishbone's front paws tore furiously through the dirt.

"Dig, dig, dig," Wishbone called out as he watched the hole before him grow deeper and deeper. "Let's see . . . there's the squeaky toy . . . and, yes, a paperback I've been saving to chew on some rainy day. No one loves books more than I do. But I don't see that bone I'm looking for. . . . It must be down there somewhere."

The white-with-brown-and-black-spots Jack Russell terrier was digging through a flower bed in the front yard of the house of his neighbor, Wanda Gilmore. It was a fine autumn afternoon, perfect digging weather. The skies were clear, the sun was bright, and all around him colored leaves floated gracefully to the ground. There was just a hint of a chill in the air. That told the dog Halloween was right around the corner.

Halloween was one of Wishbone's favorite holidays. It meant candy, costumes, and maybe a few wonderfully fun and spooky adventures.

"Ah, yes," Wishbone said, keeping his eyes on the

deepening hole. "There's half of a rubber ball. I can use that for something, I'm sure. But where is that doggone bone?"

Suddenly, Wishbone heard footsteps approaching. Scary footsteps. Wanda's footsteps!

Wishbone whipped his head around to see Wanda Gilmore walking straight toward him. Wanda was tall and slim. She had short hair, and sharp features on her face. She was a lively woman with lots of unusual habits and interests. She also had very colorful clothes. At the moment, she was wearing a strange housecoat with flower designs on the lapels.

Wanda's yard contained the freshest dirt for digging in the entire town of Oakdale. Unfortunately, Wanda believed the flower beds were to be used only for flowers—not for digging. As a result, Wishbone and Wanda had a lot of arguments over who owned the flower beds.

Do I have time to make a quick getaway? Wishbone thought as he looked around, figuring his chances of escape. *Nope, I think it's too late.*

Wanda crouched down right beside the dog. Wishbone bent back his ears, ready for the worst. Any second now, Wanda would wag an angry finger in his face. Then she would deliver a lecture on what a bad dog he had been.

Instead, to the dog's surprise, Wanda reached over and ruffled the fur on his head. "Oh, that's a good doggie," she said in a childlike tone of voice. "Yes, you are. You're the sweetest little doggie in the whole wide world, aren't you?"

With a cheery smile, Wanda stood up and waved farewell. She headed toward the Talbots' house, next door, which was where Wishbone lived. Wanda seemed to be sort of skipping as she went.

Wishbone stared after her, his brown eyes wide with

shock. *Wow! She's in a great mood today. I've never seen her like that before. She didn't even yell at me for digging in her flower bed. In fact, she was being real nice to me. Hmm . . . I don't know if this is a good thing or not. It's so weird. I better investigate this situation further.*

Wishbone ran around to the backyard of the Talbots' house. He entered the kitchen through his doggie door. Wishbone lived in the house with his best buddy, Joe, and Joe's mother, Ellen. At the moment, Ellen was taking drinking glasses out of a cabinet. She was a slender woman with thick brown hair. Besides being a librarian and amateur writer, she was a regular magician in the kitchen.

Wishbone noticed that Wanda was in the kitchen, too.

Wishbone nudged Ellen's leg and whispered, "Pssst! How is she? Is she back to normal? I mean, as normal as she gets. Come on, Ellen, tell me—this is important!"

Ellen set the glasses on the counter, not seeming to hear the question.

Why is it that no one ever listens to the dog? Wishbone thought with a sigh.

Wishbone turned his head toward Wanda. She was staring at a pair of very cool-looking sunglasses with a dreamy expression on her face.

Okay, I guess she's not back to normal, Wishbone thought.

"All right, Wanda," Ellen said as she went to the refrigerator. "You've kept me in suspense long enough. Now, what is this big secret you mentioned on the phone? Come on, you said you had to come over right away and tell me."

Wishbone cocked an ear.

"Well, last night," Wanda said, staring at the sunglasses, "I went to Pepper Pete's Pizza Parlor. The restaurant was holding its annual talent show. I was looking for some entertainment. I thought it might be fun."

Ellen listened carefully. She pulled out a pitcher of lemonade. "Ah, live entertainment," Ellen said, as she poured out two glasses. "Did you take Bob Pruitt?"

Wishbone lifted his ears a bit higher. He knew Bob Pruitt was Joe's sixth-grade English teacher at Sequoyah Middle School. Wishbone also happened to know that Wanda and Mr. Pruitt had been recently dating each other.

Wanda made a slight frown at the mention of Mr. Pruitt's name. "No, I went alone. I like anchovies on my pizza, and Bob doesn't. Besides, I don't think Bob would enjoy a talent show at Pepper Pete's."

"Why not?" Ellen asked, as the two women took their lemonade to the kitchen table and sat down. "It sounds like a good time."

Wanda took a sip of lemonade, then said, "Well . . . Bob likes more . . . you know . . . intellectual forms of entertainment. He always invites me to poetry readings and classical-music concerts—those kinds of things."

"But you like those sorts of activities, too," Ellen pointed out.

Wanda reached down to a plate on the table and picked up a cream-filled cookie. "Sure I like those sorts of activities. But sometimes I just want to . . . well, be a little different. You know, cut loose and be a bit wild."

Wanda pulled the cookie apart. She looked at each half. Then she licked the cream off one side.

Wishbone raised himself up on his hind legs. "Hey! I like to cut loose, too. In fact, since you seem to like me so much today, how about cutting loose some of that cookie?"

Wanda continued to lick the cookie as if she hadn't heard Wishbone's request.

Wishbone took a seat right beside Wanda. He figured he could stay nearby in case some cookie crumbs fell to the floor.

Just then, the back door opened. Joe Talbot stepped into the kitchen, carrying a basketball. He was a twelve-year-old boy with straight brown hair and a great smile. Not only was he a top athlete and terrific guy, but he was Wishbone's very best friend in the world.

"Hey, Joe," Wishbone said, turning away from the cookie. "How's it going, buddy?"

Joe was followed into the kitchen by David Barnes. He was Joe's age and he lived right next door, on the side opposite from Wanda's house. David had curly black hair and large, curious eyes. The boy was a top scientist and inventor. He even had a really cool laboratory right in his parents' garage.

After greeting Ellen and Wanda, Joe and David wasted no time in pouring themselves some lemonade. Wishbone's sensitive nose picked up a strong scent of sweat. He figured the boys had been having a good basketball workout.

Wishbone turned his attention back to the cookie and the talk between Ellen and Wanda.

Wanda gave Ellen a sly smile. "Anyway, Ellen, it turned out to be a good thing that I went to Pepper Pete's alone."

"And why is that?" Ellen said, leaning forward.

"You get more pizza when you don't have to share," Wishbone commented.

"I was enjoying my pizza," Wanda told Ellen. "And I was watching the talent show. It was okay, but nothing terribly exciting. A baton twirler, a tap-dancer, a ventriloquist—that kind of thing. Then *he* got up on the stage!" Again, that dreamy look came across Wanda's face. "He was a real rock-and-roll sensation! He was a lot like Elvis Presley, but even better!"

Better than Elvis? Wishbone thought doubtfully. He knew that Elvis Presley had been one of the greatest rock-and-roll performers of all time.

"And here's the best part," Wanda said, grabbing Ellen's arm. "He was looking straight at me during his entire song. He just burned a hole in me with his eyes. Well, I couldn't see his eyes because he was wearing sunglasses. But I just know they were burning a hole in me."

"Oh, Wanda, that's so exciting!" Ellen said, patting Wanda's hand. "Did you have a chance to meet him after the show?"

Wanda held up her cool-looking sunglasses. "No, I didn't meet him. But at the end of his performance, he jumped off the stage and tossed me these sunglasses! In this really neat voice, he said, 'These shades are for you, darlin'. Then, before I could say a single word . . . he disappeared."

"I think he must like you," Ellen said with a smile.

"I think so, too," Wanda said, with an even bigger smile.

Wanda and Ellen both giggled as if they were schoolgirls. Joe and David, who had been watching them, exchanged a curious look.

Wanda slipped on the sunglasses. They curved around her face, making her look a bit like a gigantic insect.

"What's this rock-and-roller's name?" Ellen asked Wanda.

"His name is Lou Dublin," Wanda said in a dreamy way. "Naturally, he won first prize at the talent show. And here's the best part. Pepper Pete's is having him back for an additional solo performance tomorrow night. Ellen, I *have* to be there. I just *have* to see him again!"

"Oh, of course you do!" Ellen said with excitement.

"So we'll all go together?" Wanda said. "You, me, Joe, David, and Sam. My treat, of course."

"Hey! I wouldn't mind going along, too," Wishbone said. "Pizza, of course, is a favorite of mine."

No one seemed to hear this remark.

Ellen shook her head. "Wanda, I'm afraid tomorrow is a school night."

"Oh, please!" Wanda begged. "This is really a special occasion. And I'm just so nervous about seeing him again. I could really use some emotional support."

"You can count on me," Wishbone said. "I never miss a chance to give emotional support—especially if there's free food."

"Yeah, Mom, let's go," Joe called over.

Ellen thought a moment. "Well, all right, Wanda. We'll go. But we'll have to make it an early night."

"Right, of course," Wanda said, as she sprang up with excitement. "Thank you so much, Ellen. We're going to

13

have a wonderful time. And you guys can have all the pizza you want!"

"You can count me in. I'll call Sam and see if she can go," David said with a pleased look.

"Uh . . . does this open invitation include me, too?" Wishbone asked Wanda.

Suddenly Ellen got up and grabbed Wanda's arm. "Oh, Wanda, wait a minute. I thought you told me a few days ago that you have a date with Bob Pruitt tomorrow night."

Wanda groaned as she pulled off the sunglasses. "Oh, that's right. We were supposed to go to that poetry reading together. I forgot all about it. Well, I'll just have to cancel on Bob. That's all there is to it. So . . . see you folks tomorrow, then. The show starts at seven-thirty, so we should get there by seven. I want to make sure we get front-row seats."

Wishbone nudged Wanda's leg. "And . . . uh . . . you *did* say that invitation includes me, didn't you? Remember how much you like me these days. All you have to do is say the word, and I'll be there with bells on. Well, maybe not bells. Maybe just a dog collar that jingles."

Wanda slipped the sunglasses back onto her face. "Well, so long, everyone. And remember, tomorrow night we are going to rock and roll!"

Wanda danced her way across the kitchen and did a happy spin. Then she left through the door. The only problem was that she had accidentally opened the door to the *broom closet*.

"Uh . . . Wanda, that's the broom closet," Ellen said at about the same time Wanda made the discovery for herself.

Joe and David laughed.

"Right. I knew that," Wanda said with a slight look

of embarrassment. "But I'm just so excited right now I can't even see straight."

"And I don't think those sunglasses help at all," Wishbone remarked.

With a giggle, Wanda left through the correct door.

Ellen, Joe, and David were all smiling at Wanda's strange behavior.

"Wow!" Ellen said to the boys. "She seems to really like this guy."

Suddenly, Wanda stuck her head back into the kitchen. She looked right at Wishbone and smiled. "Oh, I almost forgot. I'll make it a point to bring some leftover pizza crust home to Wishbone. 'Bye-bye!"

Then Wanda was gone.

Wishbone turned to Joe. "Joe, I just want to make sure I got this right. Didn't Wanda say, 'I'll make it a point to have Wishbone sit just to my left at the table'?"

Joe was already busy talking with his mom and David.

Wishbone sat down and gave his side a thoughtful scratch with his back paw. *Yes, I'm pretty sure that's what she said. This is strange. Wanda doesn't yell at me for digging in her flower bed. And then she gives me a big smile. Then, if I'm not mistaken, she just invited me along for some pizza tomorrow night! Cool! Let's hear it for rock-and-roll!*

Wanda is not acting like herself. In fact, she's acting like a different person. Of course, everyone gets a little strange once in a while. But with Wanda, we are talking about the difference between night and day . . . cats and dogs . . . Dr. Jekyll and Mr. Hyde.

Oooh! The very thought of those two names makes all the fur on my tail stand on end. Why? Because those names come from one of the scariest stories ever written.

Suddenly, I'm reminded of foggy London streets, and a frightening man who uses a cane, and a very mysterious chemical potion. The story was written in 1885 by that great master of storytelling, Robert Louis Stevenson.

The title of the book is, of course, *Strange Case of Dr. Jekyll and Mr. Hyde!*

CHAPTER TWO

Wishbone entered the foggy world of imagination. He pictured himself as Gabriel John Utterson, a respected lawyer who lived in London during the later part of the 1800s. Mr. Utterson led a completely quiet and predictable life, until . . .

On a fine, bright winter's afternoon, Gabriel John Utterson was exercising his four legs by taking a walk with his cousin, Richard Enfield. Though the two men enjoyed each other's company, they were nothing alike. Enfield was a stylish man about town, while Utterson kept his nose buried in business. Enfield was tall and youthful, but Utterson was middle-aged and somewhat low to the ground. Enfield was clean-shaven; Utterson was . . . not. Yet, the two walked together every Sunday afternoon.

As he walked, Utterson kept an eye on the flow of activity around him. This was partly from interest, and partly because he feared having a paw accidentally stepped upon. The two cousins were in a nice area of town. Most of the people were very well dressed. The men wore fancy suits, many of them topped with tall top hats upon their heads. The women wore billowing, ankle-length dresses. Their upswept hair was decorated with fancy combs and bonnets, some with feathers. Every so often, a horse-drawn carriage would go clip-clopping by, and the horses' hooves sounded loudly on the cobblestone paving.

Everything looked the same as always, and that was fine with Utterson. He liked things to stay the same, and that was how he had been living all of his fifty years. Indeed, if he could not have his tea and dog biscuits every day at exactly 4:05 in the afternoon, he felt uneasy. Not surprisingly, Utterson had never married. He also had only a few friends, and he spent little time seeking entertainment. Most of his hours were spent working for his clients and maintaining his fine reputation as a well-respected lawyer.

Utterson felt a twitch in his little black nose. It was very sensitive to smells. Today the air was full of soot. The soot came from chimney smoke. It was one of the most widespread odors of Victorian London.

Time out, here. "Victorian" refers to a time in England when a lady named Victoria was queen. And she was a queen for a *long* time! From 1837 to 1901, to be exact. Many of the world's most hair-raising tales take place in Victorian England. Just to name a few—*Dracula, Oliver Twist*, and most of the *Sherlock Holmes* stories.

Utterson found himself pausing by the window of Alexander's Butcher Shop. He was glad the shop was closed, so he wouldn't be tempted to buy anything. Even so, he desired a brief look. Magnificent cuts of meat hung on display. Utterson's eyes landed on a chain of reddish-brown sausage links, joined together by a string. The lawyer knew that every one of the long, thick sausages was stuffed with delicious pork, bread, and spices. He could almost detect their scent coming through the window. Utterson licked his chops, feeling his mouth water all the way along his tongue.

Control yourself, Utterson reminded himself. *These sausages are much too rich for your diet. Besides, what would people think of you—your reputation—to be seen drooling!*

"They look tasty, don't they?" Enfield said, flashing a smile.

"Oh, they look acceptable," Utterson replied. "Let us continue our walk."

Utterson watched his cousin start to cross the street. The young Enfield was twirling his walking stick and wearing his rounded derby hat at a stylish slant. The lawyer looked both ways before crossing the street. Not seeing or hearing the approach of horses, the lawyer followed his cousin across the cobblestones.

The two men turned the corner and began to walk along a street lined with beautiful homes. Enfield tipped his hat to a lady, and Utterson stepped out of the way of some children at play. At the end of the block, Enfield came to a stop. He pointed his cane across the street and said, "I say, Gabriel, do you see that door over there?"

Utterson turned his head. Enfield was pointing at a two-story brick building with no windows. At least there were no windows on the side that faced the corner. The bricks were time-worn, dirty, and gray. They made the building seem far more threatening than the neighboring homes. The door that Utterson spoke of was black and weather-beaten.

"Yes, I see the door," Utterson told his cousin.

"Well, it is connected in my mind with a very odd story," Enfield said.

"I'm sure it's very interesting," Utterson replied. "But I'm afraid my schedule doesn't allow time for me to stop and hear a story about this particular door."

Enfield tapped Utterson with his cane. "Oh, of course you have time, Gabriel. It's Sunday. Besides, aren't you just a little bit curious?"

"Curiosity killed the cat," Utterson remarked.

"Yes, but you are not a cat," Enfield pointed out. "Now, I insist you hear my story."

"Oh, very well," Utterson said with a sigh.

"It was very late one night, not too long ago," Enfield began. "I found myself on this street. I was staggering home from a night of dancing and such. You know how it is. Well, perhaps you don't. . . .

"Anyhow, I saw a man walking along at a good pace. Then, running from the opposite direction, I saw a young girl. She was no more than ten years of age. Well, at that corner we just turned, the girl accidentally ran straight into the man. Then the man trampled right over the girl. He left her screaming most horribly."

"What an awful thing," Utterson said.

"I thought so, too," Enfield continued. "So I ran after the man. I grabbed him by his collar, then brought him back to the spot where the poor girl lay in the street. By this time, the girl's family and several other people were gathered around the scene. The girl was more frightened than injured. But myself and all the rest, we were quite angry at the fellow."

"What did you do?" Utterson said, lifting one of his floppy ears a bit higher.

"I confess, we wanted to hurt him, but that was out of the question. So we told him he must hand over the amount of one hundred pounds to the girl's family. If he did not, we would make such a complaint about the event that the man's name would be ruined forever. Seeing that we meant business, the villain agreed to our demand."

"Did he have that much money to give?" Utterson asked. The lawyer knew that was enough money to buy every last meaty bone in the butcher shop.

Once again, Enfield pointed at the weather-beaten door with his cane. "He went over to that very door. The man pulled out a key from his suitcoat and went inside. Soon he came back out with a check for one hundred pounds. The check was perfectly good. The next day I myself cashed it for the family at the bank."

"I'm surprised such a villain would live in this nice neighborhood," Utterson commented.

Enfield lowered his voice to a whisper. "I do not think that was the villain's house. You see, the check he brought wasn't signed by him. It was signed by another man—a wealthy man whose name is as well known and respected as your own. Of course, I dare not mention this man's name for fear of causing him embarrassment. I fear there may be blackmail involved."

Utterson nodded his muzzle with understanding. He had met a few blackmailers in his day. These were people who dug up a scandal about a wealthy person. Then they offered to keep it a secret only if they were nicely paid to remain silent. It was a dirty business.

"Yes, I suppose it was blackmail," Utterson said. "By all means, don't tell me the wealthy man's name. But could you perhaps tell me the villain's name—the one who knocked down the child?"

"His name was Mr. Edward Hyde," Enfield answered.

Utterson's ears shot up straight. The name was

familiar to him. Now that he had heard the villain's name, Utterson made a disturbing discovery. The black door was the back entrance to a home owned by a friend and client of his.

"Hmmm . . . " Utterson murmured. "What did this Mr. Hyde look like?"

Enfield showed an expression of disgust. "He was short, stooped over a little, and maybe deformed. This man was hairier than average, finely dressed, but not at all pleasant to look at. I am not sure why, exactly, but there was something about his face that I found completely . . . horrifying . . . wicked."

"Horrifying, you say?"

"Yes, and wicked."

"And you're sure he used a key?"

"Yes, quite certain."

Utterson stroked a whisker with his paw. "My dear Enfield, your story has hit home. The fact is, I now know the identity of the other man, the one who signed the check from this Mr. Hyde. His name is Dr. Henry Jekyll."

"Yes, you're right!" Enfield said with amazement. "Do you know anything of the connection between these two men?"

Utterson stared at the weather-beaten door for a long moment. He felt all the fur along his back bristle with some unknown fear.

"It would not be proper of me to tell you what I know," Utterson told his cousin. "But I will tell you this, Richard. There is a very strange mystery taking shape before me. However, I plan to get to the very bottom of this affair as soon as possible. Shall we move on?"

At that, Utterson and Enfield continued their walk. Their routine Sunday stroll would never be the same again.

CHAPTER THREE

That evening, Utterson sat alone at his dining room table. He wiped his muzzle delicately with a linen napkin. The lawyer had just finished his usual Sunday supper of a single boiled beef bone and a bowl of water.

Normally after Sunday supper, Utterson would spend a few hours reading a legal book or something similar. But this evening he had a different idea in mind. He wanted to examine the strange connection between Dr. Henry Jekyll and Mr. Edward Hyde.

Utterson jumped down from his chair and trotted into his study. He spent more time in that room than any other. It was both his office and his after-hours place of relaxation. The shelves were filled with leather-bound books. They always seemed to be dusty, no matter how often his housemaid cleaned them. Utterson didn't mind, though. He was perfectly used to their dry, dusty scent.

The lawyer went to a cast-iron safe and turned the key in the lock. There he kept his most important papers, as well as a few highly prized leftover soup bones. After opening the safe, Utterson carefully pulled out a sheet of paper with his mouth. Then he placed it on the floor. He turned up the flame on a nearby gas lamp to see better.

Wishbone here. You see, people didn't have electricity in their homes back then. So all the inside lighting came from either candles or lamps whose flames were fueled by oil or gas. Outside, the street-lamps were lit by gas-fueled flames, as well. Okay, back to the story.

The paper Utterson was examining was the will of Dr. Henry Jekyll. Though Utterson didn't see Jekyll often, he had known the man for years and thought of him as a friend. Utterson took care of the doctor's legal business, which made the man his client. Utterson ran his eyes over the will, which had been written in Jekyll's own handwriting:

I, Henry Jekyll, M.D., D.C.L., LL.D., F.R.S., & C., being of sound mind . . .

Heavens! Utterson thought. *All these letters representing the degrees he has earned are very impressive. The man has more degrees than I have whiskers!*

The will went on to state that when the doctor died, all his money and possessions were to pass into the hands of his friend, Edward Hyde. Jekyll's will also stated that "in the event of my disappearance or unexplained absence for any period of more than three months, all my money and possessions should again go to Edward Hyde."

Utterson stroked a whisker thoughtfully. This last part had always bothered him. The lawyer had handled many wills during his career. But he had never seen one that said a "disappearance or unexplained absence." A will told a lawyer what to do with someone's property when that person died, and *only* in the event of that death. On top of this, now that the lawyer knew of the evilness of Mr. Hyde, the will disturbed him even more.

Utterson began to pace, his nails clicking loudly on the wooden floor. He spoke to himself, as he sometimes did when thinking through some difficult situation.

"This definitely appears to be a case of blackmail," Utterson said out loud. "On the one paw, Jekyll would be a good man to blackmail, because he is very wealthy. Yet, on the other paw, what could Edward Hyde be blackmailing Jekyll for? I have known the doctor for years. He is an extremely good man. His reputation is solid gold. He gives much time and money to charity. He never goes to the pubs. And I have not once seen the man drooling over a sausage link!"

Utterson felt the need to do something. As a lawyer, he felt a need to protect his client's interests. And, also as a friend, he felt a desire to help.

Utterson stopped his pacing. "I know what I shall do. I shall pay a visit to Hastie Lanyon—at once. Lanyon is one of Jekyll's best friends. Perhaps he will know what's going on."

Hastie Lanyon speared a slice of rare, pink roast beef with his fork. He was seated in his elegant dining room, enjoying his Sunday dinner. Utterson sat across the table from Lanyon. He watched the man eat with a very healthy appetite. The sight of the beef caused a slight watering in the lawyer's mouth.

"Are you sure you won't have some of this roast beef?" Lanyon asked Utterson. "It's quite excellent."

Utterson held up a paw. "Oh, no, I've already dined. Besides, roast beef is not really part of my diet."

"Gabey, you never allow yourself any fun!" Lanyon

roared with a loud laugh. Dr. Hastie Lanyon was a big, hearty man whose face always glowed red. That was fitting for a man who liked his meat and wine. In addition to his fun-loving ways, the man was one of the most admired doctors in London.

More than thirty years ago, Utterson, Jekyll, and Lanyon had attended college together. The three men had much in common—all three were wealthy, highly respected, and still bachelors. Though Utterson didn't socialize much with either man, he knew Jekyll and Lanyon were close friends. For this reason, Utterson had assumed Lanyon might know something of the puzzling events surrounding Henry Jekyll.

After some friendly small talk, Utterson said casually, "I say, Hastie, have you seen Henry lately? I suppose you and I are his two oldest friends."

"Much *too* old, if you ask me," Hastie said with a chuckle. "But, you know, I don't see too much of Henry these days."

"Indeed," Utterson said, tapping his paw on the fine tablecloth. "Why is that? I thought the two of you got along so well."

Lanyon's face lost some of its jolly color. "I fear Henry has gone a little strange in his mind."

"What do you mean when you say 'strange in his mind'?" Utterson asked with concern.

"Henry used to have one of the finest medical minds in the city," Lanyon explained. "He invented several new types of medicines. He did wonders for many patients. A few years ago, though, Henry began to spend less time with his patients and more time doing research in his laboratory. He wasn't coming up with any new medicines, though. One time I asked him if he would tell me what he was up to in his laboratory."

"What did he say?" Utterson asked, cocking an ear.

"He told me a little about a formula he was experimenting with," Lanyon said, clearly uncomfortable. "Well, let me say, the idea behind this formula was totally shocking. I urged Henry to give up this experimentation and return to the good work he had been doing. It seemed sinful to me that he should waste his talents. We argued back and forth for a while. Soon we were having a shouting match. As a result, Henry and I do not see each other much anymore."

"I'm sorry to hear that," Utterson commented.

Lanyon took a drink of wine, then said, "Yes, it's a shame, really. We used to be such good friends. One of these days I should patch things up with the old boy."

Utterson didn't believe this argument had anything to do with the Jekyll-and-Hyde situation. He knew

Lanyon practiced medicine in a tried-and-true way. Jekyll was willing to try new ideas and use more creative methods. He didn't see any more to it than this.

Utterson decided to ask Lanyon about something else. "Hastie, by any chance, do you know a friend of Henry's by the name of Edward Hyde?"

"No. I've never heard of him," Lanyon said without hesitation.

"I see," Utterson replied. He decided to let the matter rest at that. As a lawyer, he knew it would be improper for him to discuss Jekyll's business any further.

Lanyon placed a few slices of roast beef on a plate. Then he slid the plate across the table to Utterson. "Now, come on, Gabey," Lanyon said. "I insist that you take a few bites of this beef. If you don't, I shall be offended. Do you have any idea what the cook paid for it? A lot of money—I can tell you that!"

Out of politeness, Utterson lowered his muzzle to the beef and gobbled up a few bites.

If Utterson had eaten more beef, he might have fallen sound asleep once he got home. But his puzzlement over the Jekyll situation kept him tossing and turning in his bed all through the night.

Even though Utterson didn't sleep, nightmarish visions haunted his mind. He saw the street that contained the black and weather-beaten door. Now, though, in his vision, it was night and the street had no people in it. The gas streetlamps threw a scary, sickening glow across the scene. Suddenly, out of nowhere, he saw the shape of a man walking swiftly along the cobblestones. Then he saw a young girl running from the opposite direction. Before

Utterson could yell out a warning, the man and the girl collided with terrifying force. The girl screamed at a deafening pitch.

Utterson's tail flicked with discomfort.

Next, all was silent, and Utterson felt he was looking into Dr. Jekyll's bedroom. The doctor slept peacefully. Slowly, the door of the room opened and the shape of a man entered. With soft footsteps, the man moved to Jekyll's bedside and pulled open the curtains around the bed. The man shook the doctor awake and gestured for the doctor to get up. Utterson knew the man was forcing Jekyll to do something he did not want to do.

Utterson felt his tail stiffen.

Though Utterson knew the man in both visions was Mr. Hyde, the face was always covered in shadow. Utterson tried to make out the man's features, but the face remained in shadows.

As Utterson continued to toss and turn under his covers, he grew more and more curious to see Mr. Hyde's face. If he could just study the man's face, he thought, he might understand the situation a little better. Perhaps he would even feel less disturbed about it.

As a church bell rang the hour of six, Utterson threw off the covers. "I must get to the bottom of this," he barked out. "Yes, I must find this man. And so I shall. If he be Mr. Hyde, I shall be Mr. Seek!"

From that day forward, Utterson kept a close watch on the black and weather-beaten door. He knew Mr. Hyde had a key to the door. Utterson figured the man would return there sooner or later, for whatever dark reason.

The lawyer took care of his clients, of course. But

aside from that, he spent most of his free time hiding near the door. He hoped to see Mr. Hyde's face.

Utterson watched in the early morning, when men hurried off to work and housemaids beat the rugs on railings over the sidewalks. He watched again in the afternoon, when the street was busy with people and carriages rolled noisily over the cobblestones. He watched late into the night, seeing the stream of activity fade into a sleepy silence.

After a week, the watching paid off. Utterson stood in a doorway just a short distance from the black door. It was a chilly winter night, and Utterson ran in place to help himself keep warm. A distant church bell rang the hour of eleven. When the bell's sounds faded, the night became deadly quiet. There was not a soul in sight. Utterson was just about to give up for the night and seek the comfort of his bed.

Then . . . Utterson lifted an ear.

The lawyer's hearing was very sharp, and he thought he heard distant footsteps.

Utterson waited. Gradually, the footsteps drew closer and louder. There was a light, quick spring to the footsteps. As the steps echoed off the cobblestones, Utterson felt his tail wag back and forth with tension.

Oh, stop it! he thought, willing his tail to be still.

Soon a man came into view. He was a fairly short fellow, and his back was bent forward. He moved in a quick, jerky way that reminded Utterson of a monkey. A top hat rested on the man's head, and the cape he wore flowed in the breeze behind him. The darkness, however, prevented Utterson from seeing any of the man's features. The man crossed to the weather-beaten door and fished in his pocket for a key.

Yes, that must be Mr. Hyde!

Utterson crept over to the man. He nudged the man's leg with his muzzle and said, "Mr. Hyde, I presume?"

The man whirled around. At first he didn't see anyone. Then he realized that Utterson was even shorter than he was. He looked down at Utterson. The next instant, he twisted his head away so his face was shielded from Utterson's view by the top hat's brim.

The man spoke in a rough, raspy voice. "That is my name, yes—Mr. Hyde. What do you want?"

Again Utterson felt his tail wag with tension. After forcing it to stop, he said, "I see you are going into this house. I am an old friend of Dr. Jekyll's. My name is . . . uh . . . what *is* my name? Oh, yes, my name is Gabriel John Utterson. I wonder if I might . . . uh . . . well, enter the house with you?"

"The doctor is not home," Hyde said, still keeping his face turned away.

Utterson cleared his throat. "I see. Uh . . . well, yes. . . . I wonder if you might do me a small favor, then."

"What?"

"Will you let me see your face?"

A tense moment passed.

Very slowly, Mr. Hyde turned his face to Utterson. Wild hair and long sideburns peeked out from under the top hat. The eyes burned with a fiery threat. The teeth were crooked and rotting. A hint of a wicked smile lurked on the lips. A foul and ugly odor drifted off the man. So frightening was Mr. Hyde that Utterson almost felt as if he were staring into the face of the devil.

Every instinct in his body told Utterson to race away to safety. Yet he was not finished with his business. He needed to understand this mysterious Mr. Hyde.

Do not flee. Stand tall on all four legs and be a man!

Utterson cleared his throat again. "Thank you for

showing me your face. Now I shall know you, and that may prove useful."

Hyde gave a quick nod. "Yes, you're quite right. It may prove useful. Very useful. Let me give you my home address, as well. That, too, may prove useful."

Utterson was puzzled by this comment, but he memorized the address anyway.

"Do you have it now?" Hyde asked.

"Yes, I do," Utterson replied.

Hyde leaned toward the lawyer. As he neared Utterson, his awful smell grew stronger. "Now, tell me this," Hyde said with a snarl. "How did you know me?"

Utterson didn't want to bring his cousin Enfield into this situation by telling the story of the door. He decided to admit only part of the truth. "I . . . uh . . . knew you by description."

"Whose description?"

"Oh, well, we have friends in common."

"Friends in common? Who are they?"

"Uh . . . well . . . as a matter of fact, I was given your description by . . . uh . . . yes, Dr. Jekyll."

"That's a lie!" Hyde roared, showing his rotting teeth. "Dr. Jekyll never told you what I looked like!"

Hyde sprang toward Utterson. He lifted his cane high over his head, as if to strike the lawyer. Utterson could see that even though the man was small, he was quite muscular. The lawyer had no doubt that Mr. Hyde could crush out his life with a single blow of the cane.

Utterson bent back his ears and said in a trembling voice, "Oh, come, Mr. Hyde, that is not a gentlemanly thing to say."

Hyde threw back his head and released a savage laugh. "Gentlemanly—ha! Then I am no gentleman! No, sir, I am certainly no gentleman!"

Quick as a flash, Hyde spun around, unlocked the door, and disappeared inside the house.

Utterson stared at the black door for a long moment. Now that he had seen Mr. Hyde's face, he didn't understand the situation any better or feel any less disturbed by it. In fact, he felt like dissolving into a heap of bones right there in the street.

Pull yourself together, man!

As the lawyer trotted away from the door, he thought the matter through. Among other things, he wondered why Mr. Hyde wanted him, Utterson, to have his address.

Utterson stopped as the answer dawned on him. A chill ran along his furred spine.

"Mr. Hyde probably knows what's in Jekyll's will," he reasoned to himself. "Hyde may have forced Jekyll to make out the will according to Hyde's demands. That may have been part of the blackmail agreement. Hyde wants me to be able to find him so I could hand over all of Dr. Jekyll's money and possessions in the event of Jekyll's death. A death that he, Hyde, may help to bring about.

"But I still don't understand the part about the 'disappearance or unexplained absence.' Perhaps Hyde wanted that included in the will so he would have the option of hiding Jekyll's body."

Utterson's whiskers twitched uncontrollably. He realized that Edward Hyde might very well be planning to murder Henry Jekyll!

Chapter Four

Several nights later, Utterson found himself in the home of Henry Jekyll. The doctor was having a few friends over for dinner, and Utterson arranged an invitation for himself. He did this because he wanted to help his friend and client, Jekyll, escape from the dangerous situation with Hyde.

Utterson remained in the house after the other guests left. The hour was getting late. Still, the lawyer insisted on having a few words alone with the good doctor.

Jekyll led Utterson into a parlor, where a fire danced merrily in the fireplace. Jekyll's large home was modestly decorated, but done with great taste. It was also very clean. Everything was in place, and every piece of wood-work was beautifully polished. Utterson noticed several portraits of Jekyll's ancestors. Their painted faces stared across the room, as if to make sure nothing improper happened there.

Dr. Jekyll took a seat in a large, overstuffed chair by the fire. Utterson lay at his feet.

"Are you comfortable there?" Jekyll asked politely.

"Yes, quite," Utterson replied.

Utterson looked up at his friend and client. Dr. Henry Jekyll was a handsome man of a rather tall height. He was about the same age as Utterson, around fifty. There were just a few wrinkles around his eyes. As always, he was clean-shaven and perfectly groomed.

There was a sense of decency and gentleness about the doctor that never failed to touch Utterson's heart. Jekyll also gave off a pleasant scent that never failed to please Utterson's especially sensitive nose.

The two men spent a few minutes without talking. They just listened to the steady crackle of the fire. All the while, Jekyll found himself wondering why in the world Mr. Hyde could be blackmailing Dr. Jekyll. The only man less likely than Jekyll to do underhanded things was Utterson himself.

True, Jekyll had been just a little bit wild in his college years. He had broken a few female hearts. He had spent his share of nights gambling at cards. Perhaps once or twice he had drunk a bit too much whiskey. However, his ungentlemanly behavior had gone no further than that. The man had now outgrown even those minor offenses. Everyone in the city of London knew that Dr. Henry Jekyll was a man with a spotless reputation.

Utterson licked at a paw, wondering how to go about his mission. He didn't want to come right out and say, "You know, old boy, there's this really scary fellow who is probably going to murder you in your sleep." He needed a more polite way to bring up what was on his mind. If he could talk Jekyll into changing his will, that should prevent Hyde from attempting to murder Jekyll.

Finally Utterson cleared his throat and spoke. "Uh, Henry . . . I have been wanting to speak to you about a legal matter. It's about . . . well, that will of yours."

Jekyll showed an easy smile. "Oh, Gabriel, must you

hound me with that matter again? Yes, I know you don't
approve of the will. You've told me that countless times.
In fact, you wouldn't even have your assistant write it
out. I had to write it out myself and insist you take it. But,
I dare say, a man's will is his own business, is it not?"

"Why, yes, of course it is," Utterson said. "But . . .
well, you see . . . I have learned a thing or two about this
fellow, Edward Hyde."

"I know you have seen Mr. Hyde," Jekyll said with a
casual nod. "He told me so himself. And I apologize if he
was rude to you. His manners are not always what they
should be."

"You can say that again. If you ask me, he should be
put on a leash."

"Even so, I have a great interest in this man."

"Uh . . . may I ask why?"

Jekyll touched his lip, pausing before he spoke. "I'm

sorry, Gabriel. This is something I can't really explain. Nor do I think you would understand it. Nevertheless, he is very important to me."

Utterson rose to his hind legs and placed a paw on the doctor's knee. "Jekyll, you know me. I am a man to be trusted. If you have gotten yourself into some kind of trouble, I can help you get out of it. But you need to come clean with me. For example, if you've done something improper in the past, and this fellow knows about it . . ."

"Ah, yes, I see your concern," Jekyll said with a chuckle. "You fear that this man, Hyde, may be black-mailing me. But I can promise you that is not the case. No, no, no, this business is not nearly so bad as you think. In fact, it's not bad at all. And I give you my word—I can be free of this Hyde fellow at any time I choose to be."

"Then I wish you would consider doing so."

"But I don't wish to be free of him!" Jekyll insisted. "And I need to know that you will carry out the terms of my will—in the event of my death or disappearance. Can you promise me this?"

Jekyll looked at Utterson, a firm gaze in his eyes.

"I suppose I have no choice," Utterson said with a shrug. "A lawyer must carry out his client's desires. It doesn't matter how unusual they are. I can't pretend I shall ever like this Mr. Hyde. But, yes, Henry, I promise."

Jekyll returned to his usual easy manner. "Once again, I assure you, Gabriel, that neither you nor I have anything to fear."

"Well, I hope you're right," Utterson said, dropping down to all fours. "And I'm sorry to have worried you with this matter. But, then, it's a lawyer's job to worry about such things."

"And inch for inch," Jekyll said with a smile, "you are the most capable lawyer in London."

Jekyll leaned over to give his lawyer a few friendly strokes on the head. Utterson closed his eyes, enjoying the attention. He told himself that everything would be all right. He believed that Henry Jekyll was much too good a gentleman to let someone as evil as Mr. Hyde get the better of him.

Utterson opened his eyes.

He took a few sniffs with his little black nose. He was noticing something quite bizarre. It seemed as if Dr. Jekyll's hand had on it a very faint whiff of Mr. Hyde's odor.

Yikes! Are you scared yet? There are some pretty strange things going on in *Strange Case of Dr. Jekyll and Mr. Hyde.*

Come to think of it, there are some pretty strange things going on in Oakdale, too. The situation there is about to get even stranger. Right about . . . now.

CHAPTER FIVE

Wishbone darted out of the Talbots' house through his doggie door. At top speed, he ran to catch up with Wanda. She had just left the Talbots' house. Wishbone wanted to have a word with her.

I'd better keep an eye on Wanda, Wishbone thought as he ran. *I need to make sure she stays the way she is. I don't want anything to mess up those pizza plans for tomorrow night at Pepper Pete's.*

Wishbone pulled up alongside Wanda, in the front yard of her house. She was still wearing the cool sunglasses given to her by her rock-and-roll heartthrob. As Wanda approached her front porch, she and Wishbone both noticed a man standing by the door. The man was just about to ring the bell.

Wanda pulled off the sunglasses and called out, "Bob, what are you doing here?"

When the man turned around, Wishbone recognized him as Bob Pruitt—the very same Bob Pruitt whom Wanda had been recently dating. He was a gentle, pleasant man who always dressed with perfect neatness. His somewhat plump shape reminded Wishbone of a comfortably stuffed pillow. As a teacher of middle-school English, Mr. Pruitt had a great knowledge of poetry, books, and other things of a cultural nature.

With a beaming smile, Mr. Pruitt came down from the front porch and walked toward Wanda. Wishbone noticed he was holding flowers in one hand. Mr. Pruitt held out the bouquet to Wanda. Then he said, in a poetic way, "A rose is a rose, and these are for you, my dear."

Ah! Wishbone thought with a wagging tail. *This is an enchanted moment of romance. You know, these two really belong together.*

"Uh . . . well, thanks," Wanda said, as she took the flowers. Her reaction seemed to be a mixture of pleasure and discomfort.

An awkward silence followed. Both Wanda and Mr. Pruitt seemed a bit nervous.

Suddenly, Wanda and Mr. Pruitt spoke at the same time. Wanda said, "I know I said I was going to be free tomorrow ni——"

As Wanda was talking, Mr. Pruitt said, "I need to talk to you about tomorrow ni——"

They both stopped.

Again, they both started to speak at the same time. Mr. Pruitt said, "Well, anyway, my point is that . . ."

At the same moment, Wanda said, "Uh . . . it's just that something really unexpected has come . . ."

They both stopped again.

Is it just me, Wishbone thought, *or is this conversation really hard to follow?*

"I'm sorry," Mr. Pruitt said with a chuckle. "Go ahead."

"No, no. You go ahead," Wanda insisted.

At the same time, Wanda and Mr. Pruitt both blurted out, "Well, I can't make it tomorrow night."

They both looked at each other in surprise.

"You can't make it? Wanda asked.

"No," Mr. Pruitt said, looking down at his shoes. "You see, I . . . uh . . . well . . ."

"No, Bob, it's fine," Wanda said, showing a hint of a smile. "It's really all right."

Wanda seemed relieved. Wishbone understood why. She had other plans for tomorrow night. Tomorrow night she was planning to go to see the new man in her life—the rock-and-roll sensation who went by the name of Lou Dublin.

Mr. Pruitt looked as if he was about to speak. But then he stopped himself. He caught a glimpse of the sunglasses in Wanda's hand.

Wanda dropped the sunglasses into a pocket and said, "Were you about to say something, Bob?"

"Okay, fine," Mr. Pruitt said, suddenly appearing offended. "If you don't mind about not going to the poetry reading with me, then that is just fine. I imagine you probably have something better to do anyway!"

"Now, listen—" Wanda started to say.

Mr. Pruitt was already walking away in a huff.

Ah, life's little soap operas, Wishbone thought. *Mr. Pruitt likes Wanda, who used to like Mr. Pruitt. But now she likes Lou Dublin, which doesn't make Mr. Pruitt too happy.*

Wanda threw up her hands, then headed into her house. Wishbone turned to watch Mr. Pruitt climb on his bicycle, which was parked in Wanda's yard. As Mr. Pruitt strapped on his bike helmet, Joe and David came over. The boys looked as if they were about to continue their basketball workout.

"Hi, Mr. Pruitt," Joe and David both greeted him.

Mr. Pruitt was so upset at Wanda, he didn't even

hear them. He just kept muttering to himself, "Fine. Well, that is just fine. If she doesn't like me anymore, that is just fine by me." Still muttering, Mr. Pruitt began to pedal away from the yard.

"What's wrong with Mr. Pruitt?" Joe asked David with a puzzled look.

"I don't know," David said with a shrug.

"I could tell you," Wishbone told the boys, "but it's a private matter. So, instead, I think I'll go take a nice leisurely nap."

Wishbone lay curled up asleep on the comfy big red chair in the family study. He was dreaming of a thick sirloin steak broiled to a crisp on the outside, but pink and tender in the center. Even as he snored, his mouth was watering away.

"Hey, sleepy head. Wake up. It's morning already."

Wishbone popped open his eyes. He noticed Joe standing in the doorway. His backpack was slung over his shoulder. Morning sun streamed in through the window. Wishbone realized that he had slept all the way into the next day.

"Uh . . . yeah, hi," Wishbone said groggily.

"See ya later, boy," Joe said. He gave Wishbone a friendly smile. "Time for school."

As Joe left the room, Wishbone gave a big yawn. *This isn't like me at all,* Wishbone thought. *I'm usually the first one up. But I've been napping in this chair forever. If I didn't know better, I'd think I was turning into a . . .*

Wishbone caught a look at himself in a mirror that rested on the bookshelf. *Are my eyes beadier? Is my nose a little shorter? Do I suddenly have more whiskers? Is this really*

me, or am I becoming someone else? Am I becoming a . . . No! It can't be . . . a cat!

As Wishbone became more awake, he realized he was just falling victim to fear. He was, indeed, the same noble dog he had always been.

Oh, tonight's the big pizza night, Wishbone thought, as he stretched. *Let's see . . . How should I spend my time until then?*

Thirty minutes later, Wishbone peered through a classroom window at Sequoyah Middle School. The dog was standing on a bag of fertilizer that the groundskeeper had left leaning against a window. Wishbone knew he was looking into Mr. Pruitt's classroom. Though Bob Pruitt wasn't one of Wishbone's closest friends, he was a nice guy. Wishbone wanted to make sure the teacher was all right this morning.

All the students sat at their desks. But the English teacher, Mr. Pruitt, had not yet arrived.

Wishbone noticed Joe sitting in the classroom. The boy was tapping a pencil impatiently on his desk. Soon Joe turned around to talk with a student who was seated behind him.

That was Samantha Kepler, who was one of Joe and Wishbone's best friends. Sam, as she was usually known, had silky blond hair and really pretty hazel eyes. She was great when it came to artistic things. She was also one of the kindest humans Wishbone knew. She was always ready to reach out and lend others a helping hand.

Wishbone raised his ears to hear their conversation. His hearing was so sharp that he could hear people talking even at this distance. It also helped that the weather was warm enough so the window was open.

"Mr. Pruitt is never this late," Sam said to Joe. "I wonder what's going on with him."

"Beats me," Joe said. "I wonder if there's something wrong with Mr. Pruitt."

David, who was seated across the aisle from Joe, leaned over. "Maybe he's sick or something."

Suddenly, the door burst open. Mr. Pruitt stepped into the classroom. The guy was a mess. His blond hair was uncombed, his collar was bent, and his shirt wasn't properly buttoned. His face looked tired, as if he hadn't slept much the night before.

Mr. Pruitt shuffled over to his desk. As he flung down his briefcase, a pile of papers spilled out of his arms. He spent a few moments fumbling around, collecting the papers into a messy pile. Then, with a yawn, he took a seat in his chair.

That doesn't look like the Mr. Pruitt I know, Wishbone thought with concern.

Without a word of greeting or apology, Mr. Pruitt opened a thick book and told the class, "All right. Let's all turn to page one hundred seventy-six of *The Great Poets.* We will begin with the chapter on Robert Frost."

Most of the students looked confused. Sam raised her hand and said, "Uh . . . Mr. Pruitt, we already finished the chapter on Robert Frost."

Mr. Pruitt glanced down at his book and made an embarrassed sound. "Oh, so we did. Yes, that's right." He quickly turned through some pages. "Well, then, let's go to the next chapter. Page one hundred eighty-nine—the poetry of Ogden Nash."

The students seemed to be even more confused. Joe raised his hand and said, "Mr. Pruitt? I think we did Ogden Nash last week. He's the poet who wrote all those funny verses, right?"

Mr. Pruitt closed his book and squeezed his lips together. A look of anger crept into his eyes.

"Well, then," Mr. Pruitt said, in an irritated tone, "since the class seems to be so well versed with every great poet in this book, there will be an examination on all of them tomorrow. That's right, a test. I suggest you spend the rest of this hour studying!"

Groans went up around the room. The students seemed very upset by this information. Wishbone was also upset, and he didn't even have to take the test. The dog started to bark out a protest. Then he realized that he wasn't even supposed to be at school.

This isn't like Mr. Pruitt at all, Wishbone thought with confusion. *He's usually the nicest, neatest guy in the world. Suddenly, though, he's sloppy and even a little mean. It's as if he completely changed overnight. This is giving me the creeps.*

47

Gabriel John Utterson is about to creep into some awfully strange stuff himself. He doesn't have to take a poetry test, but he's about to stick his nose into some very dangerous business.

Let's trot on back to foggy old London and see what's going to happen next.

CHAPTER SIX

The months flew by, as they usually did. The cold months melted into warmer ones. Then the wind blew in the chilly ones. During all that time, Utterson made it part of his routine to stop in and check on Dr. Jekyll every few weeks. He did this just to make sure everything was all right with his friend and client.

The lawyer always found the doctor happy and looking very well. So, gradually, Utterson moved his fears about Edward Hyde to the back of his mind. He simply carried on with his routine life.

Yet Utterson's peace of mind was not to last for long. Around dawn of an October morning, Utterson lay asleep in the warmth of his bed. For some reason, he was having a dream in which he roamed freely in a butcher shop. In his imagination, he sampled every piece of meat in the place.

Finally, he came to a chain of long, thick links of sausage. The beautiful pork-bread-spice aroma teased its way into his nose, tickling his senses with delight. He opened his mouth, all set to sink his teeth into one of the tempting—

"Wake up, sir! Wake up!"

49

Utterson felt a hand touching his furred chest. His eyes opened slowly. With blurry vision, he saw his butler of many years standing beside the bed.

"Sir," the butler said with a bow. "I am very sorry to have awakened you. But there are policemen waiting downstairs to see you."

Utterson pulled the covers up to his muzzle and said, "Please, tell the policemen I am terribly sorry. I know that sausage isn't part of my diet, but it just looked so deliciously tempting. And there was no one warning me away. I figured I might take just a few very small bites. I know it was wrong, though. Tell them I promise never to do it again. Tell them that, will you? Please!"

"This isn't about sausage, sir," the butler said seriously. "This is about a murder."

Utterson rubbed an eye with a paw, slowly waking from his dream. "Oh, well, I'm very glad to hear this isn't about the sausage." Then Utterson exclaimed, "A murder!? Dear me! Who has been murdered? Tell me— was it Henry Jekyll? I knew it would come to this!"

"I don't know who it was," the butler replied. "You need to talk with the policemen. I will fetch your robe, sir."

Utterson put on his robe. Then he trotted down the stairs, soon entering the hallway. Two men were waiting there. The younger man wore the dark blue uniform and high, rounded hat of a police officer. The slightly older man was very tall, with sharp eyes and a neatly trimmed moustache. He wore no uniform, but an inexpensive suit.

The man in the suit gave a respectful bow and said, "Mr. Utterson, this is Sergeant Stuart. And I am Inspector Steele of Scotland Yard."

Yikes! Why are we suddenly in Scotland? The answer is, we're not! "Scotland Yard" is the name of

the headquarters of the London Metropolitan Police. It goes by that name because the original headquarters building was located on a narrow lane named "Scotland Yard." Scotland Yard has had the reputation for having the world's finest detectives.

"What seems to be the matter?" Utterson asked the inspector from Scotland Yard.

"A man was brutally murdered during the night," Inspector Steele said grimly. "Not too many hours ago. We don't know the victim's identity yet. But we discovered a letter in his pocket. It's addressed to you—'Gabriel John Utterson, attorney at law.' We thought you should be the one to open it."

The inspector handed the letter to Utterson. With a trembling paw, Utterson broke the seal of wax on the envelope. Utterson quickly removed the letter and looked it over.

The letter concerned a routine legal matter. It was not from Jekyll, but from another of the lawyer's clients. Though Utterson felt some relief that Jekyll had not been the victim, he felt sorrow over the other man's death.

"The victim's name is Sir Danvers Carew," Utterson told the inspector. "A man of high position and reputation in London. He was much loved and shall be missed by many. This letter is addressed to me because I am the man's lawyer."

"Ah, Sir Danvers Carew," the inspector said, almost showing a smile. "Yes, I have heard the name many times. An important man. Indeed, it will be quite a feather in my cap if I can bring the murderer to justice."

"Do you know the details of the murder?" Utterson asked.

Inspector Steele made his face appear more serious. "Yes, we do know. A maidservant witnessed the whole

51

incident from an overhead window. She was gazing at the sky, enjoying a view of the moon. She saw an elderly chap with white hair walking along. I now know this had to be Sir Danvers Carew. Soon, another man, a younger fellow, came along. The elder man went over to the younger one and asked a question. The maid figures he was seeking directions to some location."

"And then what?" Utterson asked, raising his ears.

"Everything seemed innocent enough," the inspector went on. "But then, all of a sudden, the maid says that the younger man burst into a great flame of anger. He stamped his feet and waved around a cane that he carried."

Though the house was quite warm, a chill ran down Utterson's furred spine.

The inspector continued. "The elderly man stepped backward, as if very much surprised. At that, the younger man went wild. He began to club the older man with his cane. When the victim fell to the ground, the younger man continued to club him in an uncontrolled rage. Then, as if that wasn't enough, the young man kicked and trampled the victim. He broke practically every bone in the old man's body. At this point, the witness at the window fainted."

Utterson asked the next question, already fearing the answer. "By any chance, do you know the murderer's name?"

"That's the lucky part," the inspector said with a wolfish grin. "A beam of moonlight fell on the man's face. The maid thought she recognized him. She thought it was a man who had once visited her master. Of course, we'll need more proof than this to convict the fellow, but I'm sure that we will get it. Oh, yes—the man's name is Edward Hyde."

Utterson felt as if his blood were turning ice-cold.

For the first time, the uniformed policeman spoke. "Not only do we think we know the man's name," he said with youthful pride. "We've also got our hands on part of the murder weapon!"

Utterson noticed that the policeman was holding half of a broken walking stick. It wasn't the same one Hyde had waved around when Utterson met him, though. This cane was much thicker, and of a most unusual design. Utterson felt all the fur along his tail bristle. Not only was this cane the weapon of a man's destruction—it was a cane that Utterson had given as a Christmas gift to Henry Jekyll a few years back.

In a hoarse voice, Utterson managed to say, "Have you been able to capture Mr. Hyde?"

"No, but we will," the inspector bragged. "Even as we speak, I've got men out searching to locate his address. I doubt he'll be there, but a good search might turn up some evidence that he's really our man."

"Perhaps I can be of assistance," Utterson offered. "A number of months ago, Mr. Hyde told me his address, and I memorized it. Perhaps he still lives there."

Inspector Steele was pleased. "Excellent! Suppose you put on some clothes and take us there!"

As soon as Utterson dressed, he and the two men from Scotland Yard climbed into a cab.

Cab? **How could they have cabs back then if they didn't even have cars? The fact is, the "cabs" used in Victorian England were horse-drawn carriages. The driver sat on a bench above and behind the horse, or horses. The passengers sat behind the driver in a little covered area.**

There were also horse-drawn buses in London back in the 1800s; they were known as "omnibuses." Some wealthy people, of course, owned their very own

private carriage. All these carriages often created big traffic jams in large cities like London.

The cab driver cracked his whip sharply. The cab began to clatter at high speed through the streets of the city. The morning fog was so thick that Utterson could barely see two feet in front of his muzzle.

London was famous for its thick fog, but this morning was much foggier than usual. The hazy vapor swirled around everywhere, as if a gigantic ghost were attempting to block the world from Utterson's view. The fog seemed to change its look as the cab traveled from one neighborhood to the next. First it was as black as tar. Then it shifted into a dark chocolate shade. Next, it changed into a floating gray smoke.

Finally, at Utterson's instruction, the cab entered the section of London commonly known as Soho. There the fog lifted a little, but Utterson was almost sorry it had. It was not a pleasant part of town. Its sights offended Utterson's eyes and made his tail twitch.

Cobblestones were soiled with mud and garbage. Ragged children huddled in grimy doorways. Men and women just stood around aimlessly, wasting the day. It seemed that almost every other building contained a pub. The stale stink of liquor shot up Utterson's sensitive nose.

The gloomy surroundings and gloomy fog and gloomy news of the murder all put the lawyer in a state of mind that was, well, gloomy.

The cab stopped. Its passengers got out and walked up to a grimy building. The address matched the one given to Mr. Utterson by Mr. Hyde. Utterson knocked on the door.

A woman with messy gray hair and cheap-looking clothing answered the door. She gave an irritated look at the inspector and the policeman. Then she looked down at Utterson. The lawyer could see the poor woman was missing half her teeth.

"Is this the home of Edward Hyde?" Utterson asked politely.

"What if it is?" the lady asked rudely.

"I'll take that to mean yes," Utterson said. "I will also assume that you are the landlady who rents him his rooms. Can you tell me if Mr. Hyde is currently at home?"

"No, he's not," the woman said. She seemed to become more irritated. "He came home late last night. Then he left again within an hour."

"Do you know where he might have gone?" asked Utterson.

The lady leaned toward Utterson. Her foul breath left him speechless. "Listen, mister, I don't make it my business to know his business. The man pays me very well. That's good enough for me. Besides, he's not even here much."

"What do you mean, 'he's not even here much'?" Utterson asked, backing away from her. "Does he live here, or not?"

"He lives here only sometimes," the lady said. "He'll come in for a couple of nights. Then I won't see him again for a month or so. Now, that's all I'm going to say. I've said too much already."

"I fear you haven't," Utterson said firmly. "You see, this man committed a murder last night. Scotland Yard is investigating the crime. That's why these men are here with me."

A look of horror crossed the woman's face. "Oh, Lord have mercy!" she whispered, mostly to herself. "The man is a murderer. I can't say I'm all that surprised."

Inspector Steele stepped forward. "Why is that?"

"If ever I saw evil stamped on a man's face"—she shivered—"it was on the face of Edward Hyde."

"That may be," the inspector said. "But we'll need better evidence than that if we are to convict this man in a court of law. May we please search through his rooms?"

"Oh, I suppose so," the woman said with a tired shrug. "Follow me."

The woman led the men inside. Then she showed them up a flight of stairs to the third floor. Using a key, she admitted the men into the rooms of Edward Hyde. She left them to their work.

The rooms were decorated with great luxury, which was surprising in that part of town. Velvet curtains covered the windows. Colorful paintings hung on the walls. Much of the furniture was carved with fancy designs. Utterson noticed that even the carpet felt especially soft under his paws. Obviously, a great sum of money had been spent on the place.

"If this Hyde fellow is in the blackmailing business," Utterson remarked, "he must be very good at it. Should I ever need a professional blackmailer, he would be the first person I would call."

The two men from Scotland Yard looked at the lawyer suspiciously.

Utterson gave an irritated sigh. "I assure you, gentlemen, that was only a joke. I would not see someone blackmailed for all the pork chops in Vienna!"

Hmm . . . suddenly, I smell food in here, Utterson thought.

Utterson sniffed the air. He caught the leftover scents of a gourmet meal from the night before: roasted pheasant, buttered potatoes, oily oysters, cream-filled pastries, nicely aged wine. The lawyer felt his mouth watering.

Don't you dare drool in front of these policemen! he quickly scolded himself.

Room by room, the three men began to search

around the place. They hoped to uncover some concrete proof that Edward Hyde had murdered Sir Danvers Carew. When they came to the bedroom, Utterson went to a top hat that lay on the carpet. He gave it a sniff. His black nose twitched as he picked up Hyde's foul, ugly odor. The hat also seemed to carry the sickening smell of dried blood.

"Inspector, look at this!" the uniformed policeman cried out.

Utterson turned to see the policeman pulling something out of a closet. It was the other half of the unusual walking stick that had been used in the brutal murder.

Inspector Steele gave a laugh of triumph. "Aha! That does it. We now have definite proof of Mr. Hyde's guilt—proof beyond a reasonable doubt. The steak and potatoes are on me tonight, Sergeant. I shall receive a promotion for my great detective work. Hyde shall hang at the gallows!"

"If you can find him—that is," Utterson pointed out.

"Oh, we'll find him, all right," the inspector said. He seized the broken cane from his fellow policeman.

Utterson wasn't so sure. Despite Hyde's slipup about leaving the cane behind, the lawyer sensed Hyde was a crafty man. Just as some dogs had a talent for avoiding the dog catcher, some criminals also had a talent for being able to avoid the police.

Utterson took a seat on the thick carpet and stroked a whisker. He realized that now, more than ever, Dr. Jekyll appeared to be in serious danger. It was bad enough knowing that Edward Hyde had once trampled a young girl. But it was even worse knowing that he had beaten an elderly man to his death.

Utterson was now convinced that Hyde might attempt to murder Henry Jekyll in hopes of inheriting the doctor's money. The thought of it made Utterson's fur bristle from head to tail.

Blast it! Utterson thought. *Henry Jekyll is my dear friend and client. If something terrible were to happen to him, I would never be able to forgive myself. I must find a way to help him!*

CHAPTER SEVEN

From Hyde's rooms in Soho, the men went their separate ways. Utterson hurried in a horse-drawn cab straight to the home of Dr. Henry Jekyll.

Utterson was greeted at the front door of Jekyll's house by a man known only as Poole. The middle-aged Poole had been the doctor's butler for as long as Utterson could remember. Utterson got the feeling Poole would remain polite and calm even if the house would be falling down around him.

Poole said to Utterson, "The doctor is in his laboratory." He spoke in a polite tone. "I'll show you there. Would you like me to take your hat and coat, sir?"

"Yes. Thank you," Utterson replied.

Utterson handed his outerwear to Poole. Then the butler led the lawyer down a long hallway that ran through the center of Henry Jekyll's house. The two men passed the kitchen. A few servants were in there, busy preparing the day's meals. Poole next opened a door that was at the rear of the house.

Utterson and Poole entered an outdoor courtyard with stone paving. The surface felt cold on the pads of the lawyer's paws. The courtyard led to Jekyll's offices and laboratory, which were part of another building. Utterson had never entered Jekyll's work quarters before. He was curious to see them.

After entering the second building, Utterson found himself in a "surgical theater." This was a vast room with a high platform in the center. Bleacher seats were all around it in a circular setup. There on the platform doctors could operate on a human body, while eager medical students watched from the bleachers.

Utterson's ears shifted uncomfortably upon seeing the big room. The theater was there because the house had previously belonged to a well-known surgeon. Now the room lay as silent as a tomb.

Poole and Utterson climbed a flight of stone steps and stopped on a landing. Before them stood a door covered with red cloth. Poole gave the door a knock. When he received no answer, he opened the door.

Cautiously, Utterson entered the laboratory. He let his eyes roam. The room was large, and quite messy. Shelves were sagging under the weight of books and odd-looking scientific instruments. Packing crates sat on the floor. Some of the opened ones overflowed with straw and bottled chemicals.

In the middle of the room, there was a large work-table littered with glasses, test tubes, burners, corked bottles, vials, tools, and all sorts of other scientific items. The strong odor of dozens of chemical smells shot up the lawyer's black nose.

At the back of the laboratory, Utterson noticed a black door. He realized that was the inside part of the very same door that his cousin Enfield had pointed out to him so many months ago.

A haze of light drifted down from an overhead

skylight. At the far end of the room, a small fire burned in a large fireplace. With his back turned away, a man sat hunched over on a crate, staring at the fire.

"Dr. Jekyll?" Utterson said quietly.

Jekyll, who was indeed the man by the fire, turned around. He looked much worse than the lawyer had ever seen him. Dark bags hung under his eyes. Stubble darkened his cheeks. He wore an exhausted expression.

"Hello, Utterson," Jekyll said weakly.

Utterson noticed that Poole had disappeared. Being careful where he placed his paws, the lawyer made his way across the laboratory to Jekyll. When he got there, he asked, "Have you heard the terrible news about Sir Danvers Carew?"

Jekyll nodded sadly. "A newsboy began yelling it a few minutes ago."

Now that Jekyll mentioned it, Utterson's sharp ears picked up the sound of a newsboy shouting in the street outside the very thick-walled building.

Over and over, the newsboy cried, "Shocking murder! The famous Sir Danvers Carew has been brutally murdered! The murderer's name is Edward Hyde! He's a man still on the loose!"

"It was a violent act!" Utterson told Jekyll. "But I hope this might bring you to your senses about this Hyde fellow. It should be clear to you now that he's not good company for someone like you."

Jekyll covered his face with his hands. For a long moment, Utterson feared the man might begin to weep. That certainly would not be proper behavior for a gentleman. Fortunately, he didn't. "Utterson," the doctor muttered, "I swear I will never spend another moment with Mr. Hyde. It is all at an end."

"Are you sure of that?"

Nancy Butcher

"Yes, I am quite sure."

"But suppose Hyde does not consider himself done with *you?*"

Jekyll uncovered his face and turned his tired eyes on the lawyer. "No, Hyde is done with me, too. I can prove it. Just this morning, I received a message from Hyde. I don't know if this message will do me harm or good in the eyes of the law. I will leave it in your hands and let you decide. The message itself is all I care about."

Jekyll reached in his pocket and pulled out a crumpled piece of paper. He offered it to Utterson, who took it in his mouth. Utterson dropped the paper to the floor and unfolded it. Then he glanced quickly over the contents. The message, in a clumsy handwriting, read:

HENRY,
YOU NEED NO LONGER CONCERN YOURSELF WITH ME. I HAVE FOUND A SURE MEANS OF ESCAPE. I SHALL NOT BE BOTHERING YOU ANY FURTHER.
EDWARD HYDE

One of the lawyer's ears flopped down with confusion. The letter bothered Utterson because it suggested that a murderer had recently been in contact with Jekyll. But the letter also pleased Utterson; it proved that Jekyll and Hyde were completely done with each other.

Then, again, Utterson did not know if he could trust Mr. Hyde. It was still very possible that Hyde might try to murder Dr. Jekyll.

Utterson carefully folded the letter. Then he placed it in his pants pocket. The lawyer was eager to get back to the delicate matter of the will.

He cleared his throat and said, "Uh . . . Henry, in light of recent events, perhaps we should once again consider changing your will. You know what I mean. You need to take Hyde's name out of it. You should replace it with some other person, or perhaps a worthy charity organization."

Jekyll thought a moment. Then he said, "Perhaps . . . but not just yet."

Utterson sat down. First he made sure he wouldn't place his tail in a pool of spilled acid or something of the sort. The lawyer knew it was time to get to the point with his client.

"You see, Henry, here's my concern. Now that we know Mr. Hyde is a killer, I am worried that he might . . . well . . . to put it bluntly . . . club you to death. Or perhaps he may try to murder you in some other horrible and violent manner.

"Why? So he may inherit all your money, which I know is quite a large sum. Of course, he wouldn't be allowed to inherit the money if he were convicted of Carew's murder. But there's always a chance he won't be convicted. Or, at least, he might very well believe that he won't be convicted.

"Either way, Hyde could still beat you to death. And, old chap, I dare say, that wouldn't be a very pleasant way to go. However, I believe we can remove all threat of this happening by simply removing Mr. Hyde's name from your will.

"Now, having said that, I have no doubt that you will take my advice and allow me to make the necessary changes for you."

Utterson waited for a response. He was sure that Jekyll would now do the right thing.

"The will must remain as it is for a time," Jekyll stated flatly.

Utterson gave his ear a frustrated scratch with his

back paw. *Clients can be so difficult sometimes,* he thought. *Jekyll's like a dog with a bone about this will. What can I do to help this man? What can I do? . . . I know. Perhaps Jekyll can somehow help the authorities capture Hyde.*

"All right, Henry," Utterson said. "The will remains as it is—for a time. But, tell me something. Do you have any idea where Mr. Hyde might be right now?"

"I'm sure he has disappeared."

"Yes, very possibly he has. But to *where* do you think he may have disappeared?"

"I doubt anyone will ever know."

Utterson gave his ear another scratch of frustration. "Uh . . . well . . . tell me this. Do you still have the envelope that the message came in? Perhaps the postmark will give us a clue as to where Hyde might be."

Jekyll shook his head. "I burned it before I realized who the letter was from. However, it had no postmark. It must have been delivered by messenger."

Utterson saw that Jekyll was in no condition to be of any help to anyone at the moment. The lawyer stood and said, "Very well. I believe I'll go now. But is there anything I can do for you? Cancel your appointments? Conduct some business with your banker?"

Again, Jekyll covered his face with his hands. This time he really did cry. Loud sobs burst forth, as if coming from deep inside a tortured soul.

"I'll take that as a 'no,'" Utterson said, a bit embarrassed at having seen Jekyll cry. He placed a paw on Jekyll's leg. "Do try to pull yourself together, Henry, old boy. We shall meet again very soon."

Utterson turned and carefully made his way through the cluttered laboratory. After walking around a crate, he saw something that almost made him jump out of his fur. He found himself staring at a creature who

seemed to be his exact double. Then, with embarrassment, he realized he was looking into a mirror that hung on a stand.

Why would Jekyll need a mirror in his lab? Utterson wondered. *I've only known mirrors to be in bedrooms or above fireplaces. And Jekyll is not too concerned with his physical appearance. Oh, well, I suppose it's of no importance.*

Utterson crossed the courtyard and returned to Jekyll's house. He found Poole there, standing just outside the kitchen. Catching a whiff of steaming hot turkey, the lawyer felt a sudden urge to go in the kitchen and ask the cook for a plate. However, there was more important business to take care of at the moment.

"I say, Poole," Utterson mentioned, "there was a message delivered here today. Could you tell me what the messenger looked like?"

"We've had no messengers today, Mr. Utterson," Poole replied. "Only the regular mail delivery."

"You must be mistaken."

"No. I am quite sure, sir."

Utterson stroked a whisker and thought. *Hmm . . . Jekyll said the letter had no postmark. That means it must have been delivered by a messenger. But Poole insists no messenger came, and a loyal and trusting butler like Poole would know. So how did that letter get into Jekyll's hands?*

Perhaps Mr. Hyde could have slipped it under the laboratory door himself. But that is highly unlikely. With Scotland Yard searching for him, certainly Mr. Hyde would not be so foolish as to wander around in broad daylight, delivering messages. Where did that letter come from? This is a puzzle, to be sure.

"Thank you," Utterson told the butler. "You have been most helpful."

Poole gave Utterson his coat and hat, followed by a respectful bow at the waist.

Utterson spent the rest of the day traveling around the big city of London. He had quite a bit of business to attend to with several clients. It was twilight by the time he returned home and settled down in his study. Dim shades of purple and red filtered in through the room's large windows.

Mr. Guest, Utterson's assistant, was seated at a desk, busy with a pile of paperwork. He was a scholarly young man who wore eyeglasses. As the room was darkening, he turned up the glow on the nearby gas lamp.

"Good afternoon, Mr. Guest," Utterson said, greeting the young fellow.

"Good afternoon, Mr. Utterson," Guest answered.

"Though, technically, it is already evening. I know it's important for a lawyer like yourself to be accurate in all matters."

"Yes, it is," Utterson said in a tired voice.

Utterson took a load off his four paws by sitting down. The lawyer was dog-tired. During his busy day, he had dealt with hundreds of legal matters and dodged hundreds of feet in the busy streets. Utterson had also been continuously worrying about the well-being of his good friend, Henry Jekyll.

Utterson had carried the message from Hyde in his pocket all day. Even now, though, he still had not been able to decide what to do with it.

As the lawyer scratched an itch on his side, an idea came to him. Mr. Guest never missed a trick. Perhaps he would have a suggestion about the letter.

Utterson trusted Guest. He had given him most of the details on the Jekyll-and-Hyde situation. He now brought him up to date on the most recent news. Then Utterson pulled the letter from his pocket and brought it over to Guest.

"Perhaps," Utterson explained, "I should hand the letter over to the police. Maybe I should let them see what they can learn from it. But then, perhaps, it might make Jekyll look bad. He is my client."

The young assistant studied the letter with great care. He read through it several times. After a few moments, he murmured, "Hmmmmm . . ."

"What do you mean by that 'hmmmmm'?" asked Utterson.

"This handwriting is unusual," Guest observed. "As you may or may not know, I am something of an expert on the subject of handwriting. It's a topic for which I have much interest. It seems to me that this handwriting looks like . . . No, that just can't be."

"What are you talking about?" Utterson said impatiently. Mr. Guest's attention to detail, though an admirable quality, could sometimes prove annoying.

"Mr. Utterson," Guest said, looking up, "may I have a brief look at Dr. Jekyll's will?"

Utterson muttered something about Guest being his assistant, not the other way around. Nevertheless, he valued Guest's opinion. The lawyer trotted over to the safe. He turned the key with his paw, opened the door, then carefully removed Henry Jekyll's will with his mouth.

Guest took the will and spread it open on the desk. He placed it right next to the letter from Mr. Hyde. He removed his eyeglasses and cleaned them with a handkerchief. Then he put them back on. Next, he began to examine the two documents in front of him.

It seemed that this would go on for a while. Utterson decided to sit on the floor and wait. He used the time as an opportunity to lick some mud from a paw.

The streets seem to be getting filthier every day, he thought with irritation.

Finally, Guest spoke. "This is most surprising, sir."

Utterson immediately stopped his paw cleaning. "What are you talking about? And why were you comparing those two documents?"

"I thought there was something familiar about Hyde's handwriting," Guest said with great excitement. "Then I realized what it was. It shows a definite resemblance to the handwriting of Dr. Jekyll. So I wished to compare the writing of each man side by side. The slant of the writing is different in each document. One handwriting is less neat than the other. But on most other points, the handwriting is identical."

"What a coincidence," Utterson remarked.

"Sir," Guest said, lowering his voice, "I do not think

it a coincidence. In my somewhat expert opinion, I believe that these two documents must have been written by the very same hand."

Utterson licked the last speck of mud from his paw.

"Hmm . . ." Utterson murmured. "That would clear up the mystery of how the letter was delivered. It would mean that Dr. Jekyll actually wrote it himself. Yet, then—"

Guest finished the sentence. "Yet, then it would mean that Jekyll was not truly finished with Mr. Hyde. It would mean he only wrote the letter to make it *appear* that he was finished with Mr. Hyde. Perhaps he hoped this would cover him if the authorities chose to question him about his connection to Hyde."

The twilight that was coming through the window was deepening into an inky blackness. Utterson felt a sinking feeling in the pit of his stomach.

So Jekyll and Hyde are not done with each other, after all, he thought. *The mysterious game continues, and so does the danger.*

Utterson stamped a paw on the floor in frustration. "Darn it all, Guest! I just don't know what is going on here. No matter how deep I dig, this Jekyll-and-Hyde business escapes my understanding!"

Wow! this guy, Utterson, is really having all his detective skills put to the test.

Speaking of tests, Joe, Sam, and David have to study for that upcoming poetry test. Maybe I should lend a helping hand. And Wanda also needs some help—with her wardrobe. She's trying to decide what to wear for tonight's performance at Pepper Pete's.

CHAPTER EIGHT

Wishbone watched Wanda as she studied herself in a floor-length mirror.

The dog sat in a chair in Wanda's oddly decorated bedroom. He and Ellen were helping Wanda select an outfit to wear to Pepper Pete's that night. The dusky light coming through the window told Wishbone that the night's big pizza event was drawing very near.

It's funny, Wishbone thought. *But Wanda seems more interested in what she will be wearing than what she will be eating. Maybe it's on account of her having such an interest in this Lou Dublin fellow. Boy, humans are sure odd sometimes.*

"How do I look?" Wanda asked, as she struck a pose in front of the mirror.

Wishbone tilted his head, studying the outfit. Wanda always dressed strangely, but this was one of her more unusual outfits. She wore tight black pants, and a sort of a flowing black top that glistened with red trim here and there. On her feet she wore bright red socks, and very high heels that were shiny black. Wishbone noticed blood-red polish on her fingernails.

"You know, Wanda," Wishbone offered, "it might be

72

just a bit . . . loud. Personally, I prefer to stay with the neutral colors—white, with maybe just a few touches of brown or black."

Wanda turned to Ellen. "Come on, Ellen. Tell me what you honestly think. I spent a fortune on this outfit today."

Ellen made an awkward face. "I don't know. . . . I personally think that this outfit seems just a little . . . wild for you, Wanda. Were you wearing something similar to this when you first met Lou Dublin?"

"Oh, heavens, no!" Wanda said with a wave of her hand. "I was just wearing regular clothes from my regular boring wardrobe."

"Maybe you should just stick with your regular wardrobe," Ellen suggested politely. "Obviously, this guy liked you just fine the way you were."

Wanda struck another pose in front of the mirror. "The way I normally am? Oh, Ellen, what's so special about me?"

"Bob Pruitt thinks you're special," Ellen said. "And I'm sure other men would, as well."

Still looking in the mirror, Wanda began to snap her fingers and dance in place. "Bob Pruitt is a very nice guy. But, let's face it—he's stuffy. No, my friend, tonight I must dress to impress. Tonight I will be seeing the sensational Lou Dublin. He's the king of rock-and-roll. And I am about to be crowned his queen! Yow!"

Wow! Wishbone thought, giving a shake of his muzzle. *A whole new side of Wanda has been unleashed. I gotta say, I'm not sure I like it. But if it helps me get some free pizza tonight, I will wait and see.*

Now, maybe I should go see how my pals are doing. I know they're busy cramming for their poetry test. It's going to be given tomorrow morning, nine-thirty sharp.

"Girls, have fun with the fashion show," Wishbone said. He jumped down from the chair and made a quick exit through an opened window.

Wishbone ran around to the back of the Talbots' house and let himself in through his doggie door. He checked the clock on the wall. Then he trotted into the living room. Joe and David were seated on the couch. They had their poetry textbooks spread out beside them. Sam was pacing the room, holding her opened textbook and flipping through the pages.

"Come on, guys," Sam told the boys. "We've got to really crack down on this studying. It's almost seven. We're supposed to leave for Pepper Pete's soon. But I don't think we're nearly ready for this test yet."

Wishbone walked to the center of the room and took charge. "You heard the lady," he called out. "Let's get cracking. We don't want to miss this pizza date for anything. Come on, I'll help. I'm not as familiar with poetry as I am with the great stories of literature. Still, I think I know way more about poetry than your average canine."

"Okay," Joe said, rubbing his forehead wearily. "Try testing us on another poem."

"Right. We'll do better on this one," David said hopefully. "At least, I *think* we will."

Sam leafed through her book some more.

Wishbone imitated the voice of a game-show host. "Okay, folks, welcome back to Poetry for Pizza. Here we go with our next round. I'll remind you once again that the winner of this game gets to feed the dog pizza tonight. All right, here comes our next question. It's a tough one, so tie on those thinking caps."

No one laughed at Wishbone's joke. The dog figured that was probably because they were all concentrating so hard.

Sam read aloud from her textbook:

"'Two roads diverged in a wood,
   And I took the one less traveled by
   And that has made all the difference.'"

"Okay, contestants," Wishbone said in his game-show voice. "You've heard the poem. Now, what is your answer?"

Joe brushed his hair back off his forehead. David scratched his ear.

"Oh, come on, guys!" Sam urged. "This is one of the easiest ones."

Wishbone walked over to the boys and whispered, *"Pssssst!* I'll give you guys a hint. This poet does his best work in the middle of the winter."

"Uhhh . . ." David murmured.

"Let's see . . ." Joe muttered.

Wishbone made the sound of a loud buzzer. *"Bzzzz!*

I am sorry, contestants. Both of those answers you gave were incorrect. The correct answer is 'Robert Frost'!"

"We don't know the answer," Joe said to Sam with a frustrated shrug. "Who is it?"

"Always repeating myself," Wishbone said, raising his voice. "I just said 'Robert Frost'!"

"That poem was by Robert Frost," Sam told the boys.

Just because I'm a dog, Wishbone thought with a sigh, *they don't think I know anything about poetry.*

"I knew that," David said quickly. "At least, I think I did."

Sam leafed through the book as she paced. "All right. Let me find another one I think might be on the test tomorrow."

"While we're waiting," Wishbone announced, "I will throw out a special bonus question. What great poet composed the following verse?:

"'A bone by any other name
Would smell just as sweet.'"

No one answered.

Wishbone pressed a paw on the rug. *"Bzzzz!* Time is up. The correct answer is 'William Steakspeare'!" Okay, according to my calculations, the score remains tied at zero apiece. A very tight contest—a very tight contest, indeed. I'll remind you, though, if no contestant is able to score a single point, all of the pizza goes to me. Next question, please."

Sam read aloud from the book:

"'I'm nobody.
Who are you?
Are you nobody, too?'"

"Ah, a lovely little verse," Wishbone commented.

Joe and David both screwed up their faces with looks of intense concentration.

Wishbone walked around in a circle. "Tick, tick, tick. Time is running low, boys. I'll give you a hint. This poet lived in Amherst, Massachusetts, and she didn't get out of the house much. Tick, tick, tick."

Very slowly, Joe muttered, "It isn't Emily Dickinson, is it, by any chance?"

Wishbone took off into a flying jump. "Yes, it is Emily Dickinson! Excellent, Joe!"

"That's exactly right," Sam said with a pleased smile. "The poem was by Emily Dickinson. Okay, the next—"

Wishbone's ears shot up as he heard a high-pitched beeping sound.

"That's my watch," David said, pushing a button on the watch to stop the sound. "I set it for the time we're supposed to leave."

Joe flipped his book shut. "We need to stop by Miss Gilmore's first. My mom's over there helping her get ready for the big night."

"Wait," Sam said, holding up a hand. "I'm not so sure we should go to Pepper Pete's. We still have a long way to go before we're ready for this test. Or to slightly change a line from a famous poem, we have 'miles to go before we eat.'"

"Nice one, Sam," Wishbone remarked. "Let's go, everyone."

Joe tossed his poetry book into his backpack. "We can just bring our books with us. We'll finish up our studying in the restaurant. I want to see this Lou Dublin act. Besides, Miss Gilmore is really counting on us to come along."

"What kind of pizza am I in the mood for?" David

77

said as he scooped up his poetry book. "Let's see . . . I think that I'd like sausage and peppers. Or maybe mushrooms."

"Okay, you guys win," Sam said with amusement. "We'll go to Pepper Pete's. But we really *do* have to study while we're there."

Joe grabbed his jacket. Then he turned to Wishbone, who was right at his heels. "We'll see ya in a little while, boy. Hold down the fort for us."

Wishbone chuckled. "What do you mean, 'see ya in a little while'? That's a joke, right? You know full well that I'm coming along. Wanda invited me herself. You don't think I'm going to miss out on pizza, do you? Pizza is poetry to my ears!"

Okay, it's time for pizza!

But on the way over to Pepper Pete's, what if we take a U-turn into the streets of nineteenth-century London? We'll be just in time to join Gabriel John Utterson for his usual Sunday stroll.

CHAPTER NINE

Time crept by until it was the tail end of winter. Utterson was taking his weekly scheduled Sunday stroll with his cousin, Richard Enfield. Though the air was cold, the day was beautifully clear and sunny.

The handsome Enfield tipped his derby at a passing lady. Utterson accidentally placed a front paw in a puddle of something that didn't smell very good.

The two men rounded a corner. They came to the block that contained the back entrance of Dr. Jekyll's property. A little more than a year had passed since Enfield first told Utterson the story of the black and weather-beaten door.

Enfield turned to admire another lady who passed by. As Utterson walked, he tried to shake the smelly wetness from his front paw.

Utterson's thoughts turned to Dr. Jekyll. For the past five months, Utterson had continued to stop by to see Jekyll every few weeks. The good doctor seemed to be doing better than ever. He always seemed cheerful and well rested.

He also began to return to the old ways of his medical

practice. He saw patients a lot. He also spent much time working for no pay in the city's many charity hospitals. The only problem was the fact that the doctor continued to refuse to make any changes in his will.

Utterson turned his thoughts to Mr. Hyde. The police had still not found him. He had become the most-wanted man in London.

A team of Scotland Yard's best detectives was working on the case around the clock. They were also offering a thousand-pound reward to anyone who could give information leading to Hyde's arrest.

Yet, there was not the faintest scent of the man anywhere. It seemed as if he had simply disappeared from the face of the earth.

The hounds of the hunt do not always catch the fox, Utterson thought. *And I fear this Hyde fellow is the slyest fox of them all.*

The sound of a carriage racing down the street interrupted Utterson's thoughts. The horse's hooves clattered across the cobblestones, loud as thunder.

As the two cousins neared the next corner, Enfield pointed with his cane. "Look. There is still a policeman on watch."

Up ahead, Utterson saw a young man in a dark blue policeman's uniform. The man was standing directly across the street from the black, weather-beaten door.

Utterson had never given the police the message that Jekyll had forged in Hyde's handwriting. He thought it would only bring trouble to his client. Besides, he didn't think Jekyll would be able to help the police in capturing Edward Hyde.

Eventually, Inspector Steele had discovered a connection between Dr. Henry Jekyll and Edward Hyde.

DR. JEKYLL AND MR. DOG

As a result, the police kept a constant watch on all entrances to the doctor's property.

Though Utterson and Enfield sometimes discussed the Jekyll-and-Hyde case, Utterson kept most of the information to himself. The lawyer knew it was not proper to discuss a client's affairs with someone other than the client. Even so, Enfield followed the case with great interest, through gossip and the newspapers.

"They think that Hyde may try to contact Jekyll," Enfield explained. "I suppose they think that sooner or later the villain will run low on money. Then he would return and try to squeeze some more cash out of Jekyll. If that happens, I suppose either he'll see the policemen and sneak away, or the policemen shall grab him as soon as he nears the door."

"Yes," Utterson said, after licking a piece of ash that had fallen on his fur. He was aware of this fact, and very glad of it. It meant there was much less of a chance that Hyde would stop by for tea—and an opportunity to clobber Jekyll to death. There was no possible way that Hyde could get into either Jekyll's house or laboratory.

"And there's the door," Enfield remarked, pointing his cane at the black door.

Utterson turned his muzzle to the door. He knew it led directly into Dr. Jekyll's laboratory. The lawyer ran his eyes over the building's gray and time-worn bricks. A slight chill ran through his body as he recalled his meeting with Mr. Hyde in this very spot more than a year ago.

The two cousins moved on, winding their way around the building. On that side, a few windows peeked out from the gray building's second floor. Utterson happened to notice a person standing behind the panes of one of the windows. He realized it was Dr. Jekyll.

Utterson called up, "Good day, Jekyll!"

Jekyll lifted the lower window and stuck his head out. He appeared to be in a small office that was next to the laboratory. The doctor looked less well than he had lately. His normally handsome features had a droop to them, as if he had spent many long and sleepless nights. Utterson thought he also noticed a deep sadness in the doctor's expression.

"Hello, Gabriel," Jekyll called down.

"How are you this fine winter day?" Utterson asked. "Why don't you come out and take a stroll with me and my cousin, Mr. Richard Enfield?"

Enfield tipped his derby. "Good afternoon, Dr. Jekyll. It's a pleasure to make your acquaintance."

Jekyll gave a polite nod to Enfield. Then he said, "I should like to join you gentlemen very much. But, no, I am afraid . . . it would not be wise. I fear I have a touch of some minor illness. I expect to recover in a day or so, but I must stay in and take care of myself."

"Oh, well, I understand," Utterson called up. "I am sorry to hear you are under the weather, old boy. I hope your good health returns quickly."

"Yes, so do I," Jekyll replied. "Good-bye."

Jekyll shut the window. For a long moment, Utterson stroked a whisker while looking through the glass panes at the figure of his friend. It almost seemed as if the doctor were standing behind the iron bars of a prison.

Utterson felt an unpleasant grumbling in his belly—and it wasn't from hunger. It seemed to be telling him that something was not quite right.

Enfield nudged Utterson with his cane. "Gabriel, I get the feeling you're not telling me everything you know about the connection between Dr. Jekyll and Mr. Hyde. I am most curious about this business, you know."

Utterson looked up at his cousin. "Curiosity killed the cat. Remember that, Richard."

"But I am not a cat," Enfield remarked with a smile. "And I don't possibly see how curiosity could kill me—or anyone else, for that matter."

The two cousins continued their stroll. They passed down the block and went around another corner. A few steps later, Utterson found himself pausing by the window of Alexander's Butcher Shop. His eyes roamed over the magnificent cuts of meat on display. Eventually, his eyes rested on a long chain of reddish-brown pork-bread-spice-filled sausages. The lawyer licked his chops.

Enfield knelt down to his older cousin. "Gabriel, every Sunday you stop and admire the sausages in this window. Do you ever purchase any?"

"Oh, no. Sausage is not part of my diet."

"Why ever not?"

Utterson patted his furred belly with a paw. "Sausages are so fattening, and I tend to put on too much weight if I'm not careful with my diet. Therefore, I always try to control my appetite."

"You weigh less than I do," Enfield mentioned. "And I am quite slender . . . not to mention handsome, and terribly popular with the ladies."

"I doubt I weigh less than you," the lawyer argued.

"I weigh one hundred sixty pounds. How much do you weigh?"

"Uh . . . I believe in the neighborhood of . . . well, not so much as one hundred sixty."

"And you *are* careful with your diet!" Enfield exclaimed. "That is foolish! I demand that you go into Alexander's tomorrow and buy yourself a chain of that sausage that has tempted you so much!"

"Oh, no, I couldn't do that," Utterson said with a

shake of his muzzle. "It wouldn't be right. Let us move on, please. I have a schedule to keep."

Utterson continued down the block, determined not to change his daily routine. Little did he know then, but the very next evening he would round a corner that would lead him into the most frightening episode yet in the Jekyll-and-Hyde case.

CHAPTER TEN

The following night, Utterson was trotting home from a restaurant. He had dined there with one of his wealthy clients. A light drizzle began to fall, steadily pelting the lawyer's fur with cold raindrops.

Just then, Utterson noticed a vacant horse-drawn cab clattering by. He raised a paw and barked out, "Cab! I say, cab! I beg you, stop! Do you not see me, man?"

Apparently, the cab driver failed to notice Utterson. The cab went charging by, leaving Utterson to fight the weather alone.

Realizing he was rather near the elegant home of Hastie Lanyon, Utterson decided he would pay a call. Not only would this get him out of the rain, but the fun-loving Lanyon might be just what the doctor ordered, so to speak, to get Utterson's tail wagging with good cheer. At the moment, the lawyer's spirits were as damp as the weather.

It was not to be a happy visit, though. At the door of Lanyon's house, the butler told him, "I'm afraid Dr. Lanyon is quite ill. But I will take you in to see him. Perhaps a visit from an old friend will do him some good."

"What is the matter with him?" Utterson asked.

"I do not know, sir," the butler replied.

The butler helped Utterson remove his wet outerwear. When he was reasonably dry, Utterson followed the butler down the hall. Soon he entered Lanyon's bedroom.

Dr. Hastie Lanyon lay in the bed, but Utterson barely recognized him. The big, healthy man with the glowing red face now appeared to be a ghost. He was quite pale, thin, and losing his hair. A ghostly, lifeless look hung in his eyes.

Utterson tried not to show his horror. He moved a chair over to the bedside. He jumped on top of the chair and did his very best to act cheerful. "So, Hastie, how are you these days?"

"How do I look?" Lanyon said weakly.

Utterson wasn't sure how to answer. "Uh . . . well, you look . . . oh, you look . . . you know, not too . . . To be frank, Hastie, you look positively awful. What the devil has happened to you?"

"The devil *has* happened to me," Lanyon said with a faint smile. "That's exactly it."

Utterson waved his paw. "Well, whatever ails you, I'm sure it will pass."

Lanyon shook his head sadly. "No, Gabey, I shall never recover. I am doomed to die soon. Oh, well, life has been pleasant for me—most of it, anyway."

"Please, tell me," Utterson said seriously. "What has happened to you, friend?"

After a long pause, Lanyon spoke. "This concerns Dr. Jekyll. I know you are interested in him, but I hesitate to tell you what I know. The shock of a certain recent event is what has put me in this dreadful state. I fear the shock may have a similar effect on you. Are you sure you want to hear what I have to tell?"

Yes, you make a good point there, Utterson thought. *I certainly don't want to end up looking as you do, poor man. But I must dig to the bottom of this Jekyll mystery.*

"Yes, I would like to hear," Utterson said.

With effort, Lanyon forced himself to sit up in bed. He took a heavy breath, then began. "Three nights ago, I received a letter from Henry Jekyll. It stated that he was very sorry for the disagreements between us, but that he would do anything for me, should I need him. He hoped I felt the same way about him, because he needed my assistance.

"The handwriting of his letter looked a little strange. But it was close enough to other letters I've seen of his. So I believed the message was really from Jekyll."

"Whatever did he want?"

"Jekyll begged me to drop whatever I was doing and take a cab to his house. There, Poole would be waiting for me with a locksmith. The three of us were then to force open the locked door of Jekyll's laboratory."

"Most mysterious," Utterson said, stroking a whisker. "I wonder why Jekyll was not able to go there himself. I saw him through the window of his study that very afternoon."

Lanyon held up a hand. "Be patient. You'll soon know why. Jekyll went on to say that once the door had been opened, I was to remove a certain drawer from one of his cabinets. I was to carry this drawer and all its contents to my home. At midnight the drawer would be claimed by a man acting on Jekyll's behalf."

"Did you carry out the mission?" Utterson asked, lifting his ears a bit higher.

"I was uncertain. I feared Jekyll might be completely out of his mind. His letter sounded so hopeless that my heart would not let me refuse. Yes, I did carry out the mission, exactly as requested. Now, heaven help me, I wish I hadn't."

Utterson stood up on his chair, growing very curious to hear the rest of the story. "Please continue," he urged.

"When I returned home," Lanyon explained, "I carefully examined the items in the drawer. They looked innocent enough. There was a small bottle containing a blood-red liquid with a medicinal smell. There were several sheets of folded paper, which contained piles of white powder. The powder was made up of tiny crystals, not unlike salt. The ingredients looked like something one might purchase from a pharmacy, though they were not familiar to me. I assume Jekyll had these ingredients made to his own special request."

"Is that all there was in the drawer?"

"No. There was one more item. It was a notebook that appeared to be a record of progress of some scientific experiment. I feared the experiment was related to the shocking idea Jekyll had discussed with me a number of years ago. I studied the notes, hoping to make some sense of the whole thing. But the words were scrawled in such a sloppy way, I couldn't make them out."

Utterson's ears shifted with confusion. "I wonder why those items were of such importance."

"You will see."

"Very well. And then what?"

"At the stroke of midnight," Lanyon continued, "there was a soft knock at my door. I kept the servants away and answered the door myself. I had a loaded revolver in my pocket, not knowing what to expect. There in the doorway stood an odd-looking man."

Utterson felt his tail flick with fear. "What did he look like?"

"He was a short fellow," Lanyon replied. "No more

than thirty years of age, I suppose. Strangely, his clothes were finely made, but they were many sizes too large for him. The effect was comical. I might have laughed if it were not for . . ."

"If it were not for what?" Utterson asked, raising his ears even higher.

Lanyon took a deep breath, as if searching for the strength to continue. "I have never seen a sight so frightening. He had very messy hair, crooked teeth . . . But, no, that's not the worst of it. There was something menacing . . . beastly . . . ferocious about him. Like an animal driven mad by rabies."

Utterson felt an icy chill run through his body. He knew beyond the shadow of a doubt that the man was Edward Hyde. He understood why Hyde couldn't have gone to the laboratory himself. This was because the police were still watching the area. But Utterson still didn't understand why Jekyll couldn't go to the laboratory himself. There were so many things Utterson didn't understand. . . .

"That man was Edward Hyde," Utterson informed his friend.

Lanyon's mouth fell open with surprise.

"Yes," Utterson continued. "The same Edward Hyde who murdered Sir Danvers Carew. The same Edward Hyde the police have been searching for since October. I have seen him myself. And, yes, he is truly frightening to see. But, at the time I saw him, his clothes fit him perfectly well. Do you have any idea why he was wearing clothes far too large for him?"

"You will see, Gabey," Lanyon said with a slight tremble in his voice.

"Yes, I'm sorry. Please continue."

"This man, Mr. Hyde, he grabbed my arm and asked

if I had what he had come for. I said yes, and I led him into my consulting room. The man sprang toward the drawer with a great quickness. When he realized everything was there, he released a huge sigh of relief."

"Yes. Go on," Utterson said, almost panting with curiosity.

"He asked for a glass," Lanyon went on, growing fearful as he spoke. "I gave one to him. He poured the red liquid into the glass. Then he mixed in the powder. It began to hiss and bubble, which is not so uncommon among chemical mixtures. Then it changed colors a few times, which is not so common. And then . . ."

A look of terror shot out of Lanyon's eyes, as if he was witnessing something evil. Lanyon covered his face, as if to block out the vision.

"And then what?" Utterson asked, stretching his muzzle forward.

Lanyon forced himself to lower his hands. In a

shaky voice, he said, "Mr. Hyde lifted the glass to his lips . . ."

"And he drank what was in it?"

Lanyon gave a troubled nod.

Utterson couldn't understand what would be so horrifying about a man drinking a potion. But he knew there must be more to it than he could possibly guess.

"And then what happened after Mr. Hyde drank the potion?" asked Utterson, raising his ears as high as they would go.

Suddenly, Lanyon was trembling all over, helpless to control his body. "This man . . . only the devil himself can imagine . . . After he drank . . . he changed . . . before my very eyes . . . He changed into . . ."

Lanyon sank back on his pillow, exhausted.

"What do you mean, he 'changed'?" Utterson said, practically jumping out of his fur. "He changed into what?"

Lanyon's face paled to white and he began to gasp for breath.

Utterson leaped from his chair to the bed. He gave Lanyon a few reassuring licks with his tongue. Then he said, "It's all right, my friend. Don't attempt to talk. Just relax. I will get you medical care."

Lanyon grabbed Utterson's paw. He struggled to speak, but the words were strangled in his throat.

At the top of his lungs, Utterson barked out to the servants, "Someone, please go fetch a doctor at once! Dr. Lanyon is in a desperate condition!"

Several days later, Utterson stood under a black umbrella at the funeral of Dr. Hastie Lanyon. It was a sad occasion. The day was gray, grim, and rainy. Lanyon was a well-liked man. Despite the weather, the funeral was well attended. However, one man who should have been there was not present—Dr. Henry Jekyll.

Lanyon had died the day after Utterson had visited him at his bedside. As a result, Utterson never got to hear the rest of Lanyon's strange story. That was too bad, because the story had added many confusing questions to the already puzzling case of Dr. Jekyll and Mr. Hyde.

Utterson stroked a whisker. As he had been doing since his visit with Lanyon, Utterson thought through the new questions. *Why could Jekyll not go to his own laboratory? Why was Hyde wearing clothes that were several sizes too large for him? Why was Hyde drinking Jekyll's potion? And what on earth had the potion done to Hyde?*

On the day of Lanyon's death, Utterson had paid a visit to Jekyll's home in the hope of getting some answers. However, Utterson was not admitted to the house. According to Poole, Jekyll had left orders that he would not be seeing any visitors for quite some time. Utterson asked Poole why this was, but the butler did not know the answer.

And so we add another question to the stack, Utterson thought. *Why is Jekyll refusing all visitors?*

For a complete year, Utterson's curiosity about the Jekyll affair had been increasing. Now the curiosity was so great he could barely stand it. It itched through every inch of his fur, as if he had been invaded by an army of fleas. In addition to all this, Utterson was now more concerned than ever about the well-being of Henry Jekyll.

The rain fell harder as Lanyon's coffin was lowered into the grave. Even with the umbrella, Utterson was getting soaked. He gave himself a wild shake, throwing rainwater off his fur.

"I wish I could shake off this Jekyll-and-Hyde affair so easily," Utterson muttered to himself. "The mystery must be solved, and the horror must be stopped. This business has already killed Carew and Lanyon. I fear it may kill Henry Jekyll, as well. For that matter, it might even kill Gabriel John Utterson!"

And the suspense of this story is killing *me*. So what was that mysterious color-changing potion, anyway? Just thinking about it is giving me the creeps.

And the creeps always make me hungry. What do you say we head on back to Pepper Pete's, in Oakdale, for a bite of pizza?

CHAPTER ELEVEN

Wishbone tore into a piece of delicious pizza. In a matter of seconds, the pizza was chewed, swallowed, and gone. It went so fast that the hungry dog hadn't even noticed what the topping was. Wishbone was standing underneath a table at Pepper Pete's, right between Joe and David's feet.

"Ah! Not bad," Wishbone said to no one in particular.

Wishbone stepped out from under the table and ran his eyes around the restaurant. It was crowded, and the conversation was loud. Almost every seat was taken. The walls were bare brick, the floors black-and-white tile, and each table and booth had a checkered tablecloth. To Wishbone's nose, the aromas coming from the great big ovens were out of this world. His only complaint was the menu. No kibble. *Now, where are those comment cards when you need them?*

It had been no simple operation getting to the pizza parlor. When Wishbone followed the group into Ellen's car, she reminded Wishbone that he was not going with them. This was immediately followed by a discussion between Wanda and Ellen. Within a few seconds they seemed to come to an agreement.

"You can go to Pepper Pete's," said Wanda, grinning. But Wishbone had to promise to be on his very best behavior. He had given Wanda many friendly licks for all of her help, and she didn't even seem to mind having a wet hand.

I think she needs a few more licks for her devoted actions tonight, Wishbone thought.

Wishbone went over to Wanda and gave her shoe a few licks. She barely noticed his presence, though. At the moment, she was staring at a metal napkin container, using its shiny surface as a mirror. She was wearing the same strange getup that she had tried on for Ellen and Wishbone a short while ago.

"Are you sure I look okay?" Wanda asked Ellen nervously.

"You look terrific!" Ellen assured Wanda. "Like a wild rock-and-roll queen. And that ought to be just fine with Lou Dublin."

"Oh, just wait until you see him," Wanda said, adjusting a lock of her hair. "His act is absolutely the most sensational performance you can imagine!"

"Miss Gilmore," Joe said, sliding the pizza tray over, "why don't you take some pizza? I don't think you've eaten any yet."

"I'll have some in a minute," Wanda said. She leaned close to the napkin container to check her thick eye makeup. "I'm just too keyed up right now."

"There may not be any left in a minute," Ellen said humorously. "Remember, there are children and a dog among us."

Sam tapped a fork on the table impatiently. "Come on, Joe . . . David. We'd better cram in some more studying. We did pretty well while we were waiting for the pizza to get here, but we still have a lot of material to cover. I think we might be up to speed on the American poets. Let's move on to the English poets. You do the quizzing, Joe."

"Sounds good to me," David said, with his mouth full of hot, gooey pizza.

Wishbone returned to the other side of the table and nudged David's leg. "And let's move on to another piece of pizza for the dog, okay, David?"

David reached down and set a very generous piece of pizza on Wishbone's plate.

"Thank you very much," Wishbone said. He bent his head down to devour the new taste sensation. As he ate, the dog made it a point to also keep an eye on the action going on above. He knew the kids might need some more help with their studying.

Joe, Sam, and David all had their poetry textbooks perched on the table. While holding a slice of pizza in one hand, Joe turned a page of his poetry book with his other hand. "Here goes," he said. Then he read aloud:

> "'Sunset and evening star
> And one clear call for me,
> May there be no moaning of the bar
> When I put out to sea.'"

"Oh, I love that one," Wanda said, setting down her makeshift mirror to listen. "It's such a beautiful poem. I think it's one of Bob's favorites, too."

"Uh . . . let me think," Sam said, rubbing her chin. "Is it by Shelley?"

Joe shook his head.

"How about Coleridge?" David guessed with a frown. Joe shook his head again.

"You guysh are clushing at shtraws," Wishbone said as he chewed his pizza with delight. "Shhe iff you cah count all way to—"

"Tennyson!" Sam said, pounding her hand on the table.

"Bingo!" Joe said with an enthusiastic nod.

After swallowing the last of his pizza, Wishbone said, "Yes, indeed—Alfred, Lord Tennyson. He was perhaps

the most beloved poet of the Victorian Age. Now, how about another sampling of pizza, someone?"

"Let's try another poem," Joe suggested. He turned a page, then read aloud:

> "'There's a certain slant of light
> On winter afternoons—'"

Suddenly, the pizza parlor went pitch-dark. Then wide beams of colored light began to sweep around the room. The chatter in the restaurant faded into silence.

"The show's about to start!" Wanda said excitedly, clutching Ellen's arm.

Wishbone pawed at Joe's leg. "Hey! Bring me up to the balcony, pal. I need a better view for the show."

Joe reached down and pulled Wishbone up into his lap.

An announcer's voice sounded over a loudspeaker. "And now, ladies and gentlemen, this is the moment you've all been waiting for. Let's give a big Pepper Pete's welcome for the exciting Mr.—Lou—Dublin!"

A set of double doors swung open, and the star of the evening made his entrance. A bright spotlight beam focused on him—and he certainly was a sight to see. The performer wore a tight white jumpsuit with a large jeweled belt around the waist. Around his neck he wore a cape made of a glittering red material. His hair was black, and it was slicked back on the top and sides into an old 1950s style called a "ducktail." Black bushy sideburns ran along his ears.

Mr. Lou Dublin looked very much like Elvis Presley, the legendary rock-and-roll superstar from the 1950s, 1960s, and 1970s. The entertainer of the evening even had the same plumpness Elvis Presley had in his later years.

Across his face, the Elvis lookalike wore a pair of curved sunglasses. They were exactly like the ones Wanda had worn the day before.

Lou Dublin flung his arms wide, holding out the flowing cape. He announced loudly, "Well, lookie-lookie at what the dog dragged in!"

Wishbone turned to Joe. "Hey! What's he talking about? I didn't drag anything in here."

Lou Dublin went over to a passing waitress. "Hey, there, darlin'," he said, as he twirled her around a few times. "Yeah, you're lookin' beautiful tonight. Would you run in that kitchen and bring me a double everything!"

Most everyone in the restaurant laughed. Wishbone noticed that Lou Dublin had the same deep voice and thick Southern accent for which Elvis Presley was famous. Wishbone had seen some old Elvis movies on television a few times.

Lou Dublin danced his way over to Wanda. "Yow!" he said, as he ran a hand across her shoulder. "I saw you in here the other night, didn't I, darlin'? I'd never forget you!"

Wanda looked as if she would explode with excitement from all the special attention.

The spotlight followed Lou Dublin to a small stage that had been set up right near Wishbone's table. In the background, a giant record spun in circles.

Dublin pointed at a waitress and said, "Hey, darlin' in the blue dress! Why don't you come on over here and help me with my cape?"

"You know, this guy imitates Elvis pretty well," Wishbone told Joe.

Joe didn't respond, but Wishbone figured that was because he was too caught up in watching the act.

An embarrassed waitress ran over and helped Dublin remove his cape. Lou Dublin gave the woman a big wink as he said, "Thank you very much."

As the waitress moved away with the cape, Dublin grabbed a microphone out of its holder on the floor stand in front of him.

Wishbone noticed that the entertainer's fingers were covered with jeweled rings.

Lou Dublin pointed right at Wanda and said, "Wanda, gal, this one's just for you!"

Wanda gripped Ellen's arm and released a scream.

"Wanda, please," Wishbone advised. "*Try* to control yourself."

Suddenly, 1950s rock-and-roll music blared from loudspeakers. Wishbone folded down his ears a bit, to dim the sound. With a flashy gesture, Dublin tilted the microphone to his mouth. Then he began to sing with typical rock-and-roll energy:

> "Well, well, I'm a puppy dog
> For your love!
> You make me howl
> To the moon above
> I'll come a-runnin'!"

Wishbone noticed that Lou Dublin's style was very much like that of Elvis Presley. This was especially true of the way he wriggled his hips and sometimes made a snarling expression with his upper lip.

> "'Cause I'm a puppy dog
> For your love!"

The crowd was eating up the performance. They were smiling and clapping and swaying their heads to the beat of the music. Even Wishbone found himself tapping a paw.

"Go, Lou!" Wanda squealed with delight. "You are the coolest!"

"Thank you! Thank you very much!" Lou Dublin said, flashing a bright smile at Wanda.

Dublin tilted the microphone in the opposite direction. Then he went into the song's second verse. As he made his way through the song, his performance grew wilder and wilder.

"Give me a little cuddle
A coochie-coo!"

At this point, Dublin began swinging his free arm around and around in rhythm to the music's beat.

"I'll make you smile
Can't you hear me barkin' for . . . "

"Excuse me, Mr. Dublin. *I'll* take care of the barking part, thank you. You just stick to singing your song." Wishbone knew that *no one* could imitate *his* bark.

At that point in his song, Lou Dublin began to swing his head around and around in sync with the music's rhythm. His head was finally spinning so fast that just watching it made Wishbone dizzy.

"You!
You!
You! You! You! You! You!"

To Wishbone's horror, something dark and furry suddenly went flying off Lou Dublin's head. It sailed through the air and landed smack in the middle of a pizza that sat on Wishbone's table.

At first, Wishbone thought the unidentified flying object might be a leaping cat that had somehow managed to make its way on the scene. But then Wishbone realized that the furry thing was Lou Dublin's wig!

Could that be where the saying "the fur will fly" came from? Wishbone thought.

Sounds of shock rippled through the restaurant as customers gasped.

Wanda held both her hands to her cheeks. A look of complete horror covered her face.

Wishbone whipped his head around to look at Lou Dublin, who had stopped singing. Without the fancy wig, the man no longer looked so much like Elvis Presley. At the moment, he looked exactly like the gentle, pleasant, plump, poetry-loving . . . Bob Pruitt!

Wow! This situation is getting pretty weird. Suppose we head on back through the foggy streets of London? Then maybe we'll break into the laboratory of a certain odd doctor. There, we may or may not find a murderer lurking. Come along . . . if you dare.

CHAPTER TWELVE

It was nearing midnight, many hours after Dr. Lanyon's funeral. Utterson lay on the floor of his study. His nose was buried in a thick volume of legal information. Outside, the wind lashed wildly against the trees, as if to rip them from their roots.

The lawyer's tail jumped when, suddenly, there was an urgent knocking at his front door. Utterson knew it must be some sort of emergency. No civilized person would make a social visit at that late hour. Since the servants had been given the night off, Utterson trotted through the house. Soon he arrived at the front door.

"Who is it, please?" Utterson called.

"It's Poole, sir," a voice replied.

Utterson unbolted the door. He saw Dr. Jekyll's butler standing on the doorstep. The normally calm Poole showed a terrified look in his eyes.

"What is it, Poole?" Utterson asked the man with great concern.

"Something is terribly wrong with Dr. Jekyll," Poole said in a trembling voice. "He's not exactly ill, but I know something is terribly wrong."

"Could you be more clear, please?"

"I'm afraid I can't, Mr. Utterson. But I fear there has been some foul play."

Utterson's whiskers twitched. "Foul play! What sort of foul play?"

"I dare not say, sir. For in truth, I don't know. But I was hoping you would come along with me and see for yourself."

"Very well. I will."

The lawyer threw on his coat, stuck his top hat over his ears, and hurried outside with Poole. Utterson and Poole walked at a brisk pace through the windy streets. Above, a slender crescent moon lay on its side, as if knocked over by the wind's power. The street was especially dark, because the wind had blown out the flames that lit the gas streetlamps.

"Now, tell me more of this troubling situation," Utterson urged Poole.

"As you know," Poole explained, "the doctor has refused to see anyone the past few days. He's also been spending most of his time locked up in his laboratory. But even so, he had been coming out briefly—for meals, or sleep, or to change his clothes. Until now, that is. You see, for the past day and a half, he has not once come out of the laboratory. Not once. At his request, I leave his meals right outside the door. Then he snatches them inside when no one is around."

"That is certainly most odd," Utterson said, his tail shivering with cold.

"And he's had me looking all over town for a certain medicine," Poole explained. "I go to this or that drugstore and bring back the medicine. It is a type of white powder. I slip the packet of powder under the door to the doctor, but it never seems to be the one he needs. He keeps leaving

105

notes on the door, telling me to try this and that other place. But each time I bring him a new medicine, he complains that the mixture is wrong."

"Most strange," Utterson said.

"And then this morning," Poole continued, "I happened to enter the laboratory area, bringing the doctor his breakfast. He was in the surgical theater. Well, the second I came in, he gave a startled cry and scurried away like a rat. Why would he behave like that? I have served the man faithfully for almost thirty years."

"I don't know, Poole. But I am determined to get to the bottom of this. Is there anything else?"

"Once I heard him weeping in there," Poole said with deep concern. "It cut straight to my heart, it did. It sounded to me like the cries of a lost soul."

Utterson realized he had not seen a single person since he left his house. It was almost as if the wind had swept everyone away. Never had Utterson wanted to be around people so much. Utterson wasn't sure why that was. Perhaps it was because he sensed that he was headed straight in the opposite direction—into the dark face of doom. And that thought made every inch of his fur bristle.

Soon, Utterson and Poole arrived at the front door of Dr. Jekyll's house. Poole knocked at the door. A cautious voice called out, "Who is it?"

"It's me—Poole," the butler replied. "It's all right. You may open the door."

When a servant opened the door, Utterson followed Poole inside to a parlor. Jekyll's five other servants were gathered there. The women were weeping and the men looked tense. Utterson detected a heavy scent of fear coming off each of them.

Utterson fought not to take on some of their fear. He

prided himself on being a calm man. He knew he must remain that way, now more than ever.

As Utterson handed his coat and hat to Poole, he said, "Let us go try to see the doctor. And, Poole, I would suggest you bring an axe."

Poole fetched an axe. Utterson took a lit candle from one of the servants. The lawyer gave Poole a nod of his muzzle. The two men moved through the house, soon coming outside and entering the courtyard. They passed through a door and walked through the surgical theater. Next, they climbed the stone steps leading to the red door of Jekyll's laboratory. The only light came from the flickering candle flame they had with them.

Poole gave a firm knock and then called out, "Sir? Mr. Utterson is here, asking to see you!"

"Tell him to go away!" a voice shouted back, thick with anger. "I cannot see anyone right now!"

Still holding the axe, Poole looked to Utterson for guidance. Utterson led Poole back down the steps and into the surgical theater. His tail flicked uncomfortably at the idea of being in a place where bodies had once been operated upon. Unfortunately, it was the only place to talk at the moment.

Utterson set down the candle, then whispered, "Did you notice that Henry's voice sounded different than usual?"

"Sir, I'm glad to hear you say that," Poole whispered in reply. "Because I think so, too. And here's another thing, Mr. Utterson. When I saw the doctor scurry away this morning, I caught a glimpse of his face—just for a second. It didn't look like the doctor *at all*. It almost looked as if . . . well . . . he were wearing a horrifying mask."

Utterson sat down and gave his side a thoughtful

scratch. "You know, I think I'm beginning to make some sense of this. Perhaps your master has come down with one of those diseases that deform the face. Maybe that's why he doesn't want to be seen. Perhaps, as you say, he was wearing a mask to hide the problem. Indeed, such a disease might even have changed his voice. This would also explain the doctor's urgent need for medicine. I'll admit this doesn't explain every bit of strangeness in this affair. But it does give us at least some answers. What do you think of my theory?"

Poole knelt down to the lawyer. "Do you really wish to know what I think, sir?"

"Yes. That's why I asked."

Poole paused before speaking. "I was afraid to say it before, sir. . . . Here's what I really believe—I believe that is not the doctor in there at all . . . but someone else."

"Why would someone else be in there?"

"Perhaps this someone murdered the doctor, and whoever did it is the one in there now. In fact, the mask I saw seemed as if it might possibly be Mr. Hyde's face."

Utterson stroked a whisker. "I'll admit I've had my fears about Hyde murdering Jekyll. But I do not think that is what has recently happened."

"I do, sir."

Utterson paced around the theater, the clicking of his nails echoing off the cold stone floor. "But it's just not logical, Poole. Edward Hyde is the most-wanted man in London. There's a one-thousand-pound reward being offered to anyone who can bring him to justice. On top of that, the police know he is an acquaintance of Dr. Jekyll's. Scotland Yard detectives have been keeping a constant watch on all entrances to Jekyll's house and laboratory. There's no way that Hyde could have entered that room without immediately being captured."

Poole seemed as if he might burst into tears. "Oh, sir, I don't know what's logical or not logical. But it is the belief of my heart that this being in there is not my master!"

Utterson rubbed his muzzle against Poole's leg, hoping to comfort the man. "If that is your firm belief, then the least I can do is prove to you it is not so. I don't like the idea of invading poor Henry's privacy, but the truth must be known. Bring the axe."

Utterson picked up the candle and led the butler back up the stone steps. The two men stopped outside the laboratory door.

"Jekyll!" Utterson barked out. "I demand to see you! I demand it!"

The only reply was silence.

"Very well," Utterson barked at the door. "I have given you fair warning. I must see you—and I shall see you. If you don't do so willingly, then I will need to use brute force!"

"Utterson!" a voice cried out in desperation. "For God's sake, do not come in!"

"Down with the door!" Utterson ordered the butler.

Poole swung the axe at the door, right above the lock. There was a loud *thwack!* It seemed as if the whole building shook.

From behind the door came a piercing scream. Utterson folded down his floppy ears. The sound reminded him of an animal struggling to free itself from the ugly teeth of a steel trap.

When the scream ended, Utterson gestured for Poole to continue his work. Over and over, the butler attacked the door with the axe. The thick wood of the door splintered and chipped and split beneath the blows. At last, after several minutes, Poole was able to kick the door open.

Utterson and Poole stepped into the laboratory.

The lab was quiet and completely still. Across the room, a small fire burned in the fireplace. The flames threw eerie shadows on the walls.

Among all the mess, Utterson spotted a body lying face-down on the floor. Utterson rushed over. He grabbed the man's wrist with his paw and checked for a pulse. There was none. The man was dead. A familiar and pleasant scent hung in the air around the body. The lawyer knew instantly that the dead man was Henry Jekyll.

Utterson tilted back his muzzle and sounded a long howl of grief.

Then Utterson, who rarely showed much emotion, forced himself to calm down. He noticed an empty glass lying near the body. He gave it a sniff. His black nose twitched at the bitter aroma.

He turned to Poole, who was watching with a shocked expression. "There was cyanide in that glass," Utterson told the butler. "That is a type of poison frequently used by people to commit suicide. I am afraid poor Henry Jekyll is quite dead. Murdered by his own hand."

Poole walked over and gently turned the man onto his back.

Utterson was shocked. He found himself staring into the horrid face of Edward Hyde!

There was no question about it. That was the same evil face Utterson had seen more than a year ago outside the door to the scientist's laboratory. The face appeared more devilish than ever now. The eyes stared straight out with extreme hatred. The mouth was open but twisted; the crooked, yellow teeth gritted together. It looked as if the man had died right in the middle of a vicious struggle.

Utterson pawed at the dead man's clothing. Just as Lanyon had described, the clothes were several sizes too large for Hyde. As Utterson examined the clothes, his nose was attacked by Hyde's foul and ugly odor.

I was doggone positive that the body smelled of Henry Jekyll, Utterson thought. *At first, at least. But now it clearly smells of Hyde. Perhaps all these chemical smells floating in the air confused my nose. It can happen to the best of breeds.*

Utterson looked up at Poole. "Uh . . . obviously I was quite mistaken. This body is indeed that of Mr. Edward Hyde. Now we must do our best to find Dr. Jekyll. Let us try to chase him down at once. I only pray we are not too late!"

Utterson and Poole both rushed for the door with great haste. Before they passed through, the two men stopped in their tracks.

Poole looked down at the lawyer. "Sir, exactly where are we going?"

"That is a very good question, Poole. I'm sorry to say, but I have no idea."

"Neither have I, sir."

"Hmm . . . this presents a problem."

"Indeed, it does, sir."

Utterson held up a paw. "I know. Let's search the laboratory. Perhaps we will find some clue telling us where Jekyll might be."

"A fine idea, sir."

"Thank you, Poole."

Utterson and Poole moved around the room. They turned furniture over, picked up lab instruments, searching for any sign that might give a clue to Jekyll's location. At one point, Utterson noticed quite a few patches of white powder scattered on the floor. Being careful not to touch the powder, he followed the white trail until it stopped.

Utterson glanced up and sounded a yelp of surprise. He was staring at someone who might have been his twin. Then, with embarrassment, the lawyer realized he was staring into the mirror that hung from a stand.

I wish this mirror could tell me what happened in here, Utterson thought. *While the mirror's at it, I wish it could tell me why a mirror is in the laboratory.*

"Sir! Take a look at this!" Poole cried out.

Utterson turned to see Poole pointing to something that lay on the worktable; it was an envelope. Poole reached for it and handed it to Utterson.

It was a large envelope. "Gabriel John Utterson" was written on the outside, along with the date. Utterson's heart leaped when he realized it was the date of that very day.

"He was here and alive today!" Utterson exclaimed, his tail wagging with happiness. "Perhaps that *was* his voice we just heard. Perhaps Hyde didn't commit suicide after all. Maybe Jekyll forced the poison down Hyde's wicked throat, then escaped through that door to the street. If so, I can't say I'm all too sorry. Oh, Poole, your master may still be safe!"

Hoping to get some answers, Utterson ripped open the large envelope with his teeth. He pulled out a sheet of paper and flattened it with his paws.

It was a will made out in Jekyll's own handwriting. Poole brought over a lit candle. Utterson quickly examined the document. The terms of the will appeared very similar to Jekyll's previous will—with one major difference. A sentence read:

In the event of my disappearance or unexplained absence, all of my money and possessions shall pass into the hands of Gabriel John Utterson.

Hey! That's me, Utterson thought with alarm. *True, I was pestering Jekyll about changing the will. I hope he didn't think that it was because I wanted all of his wealth!*

"You may have just become quite rich, sir," Poole said in a dignified tone.

"Perhaps," Utterson mumbled. "But right now I would trade all the riches in the world for an explanation to this mystery."

Utterson dug a paw inside the large envelope. He discovered there was something else in there—a medium-size envelope. He wasted no time tearing it open. He pulled out a sheet of paper that contained only the following handwritten message:

MY *dear Gabriel,*
BY *the time You read this, I shall have disappeared under the most mysterious circumstances. You will never find me or my body, but I can assure You that I exist no more. You may leave it at that. Or, if You wish to know the entire truth, read the letter enclosed in the small envelope.*

HenrY

Utterson again dug inside the original large envelope. Sure enough, he found a small envelope. It was sealed in several places with wax. Eagerly, greedily, Utterson opened the envelope, but then . . . he stopped himself.

For a complete year, Utterson had been digging and digging into the mystery of Dr. Henry Jekyll and Mr. Edward Hyde. However, now that the full truth lay temptingly beneath his paws, he realized he wasn't sure he wanted to know it. Utterson felt quite certain that the solution to this mystery would be more terrifying than anything he could ever imagine.

Where in the world is Dr. Jekyll? Tell me that! And while we're asking questions, why in the world is Mr. Pruitt pretending to be Lou Dublin?

Hopefully, we will soon dig up some answers to these two doggone mysteries. . . .

CHAPTER THIRTEEN

With very wide eyes, Wishbone gaped at Bob Pruitt. The man stood onstage, dressed as the rocker Lou Dublin. Without the black wig, Mr. Pruitt's face and blond hair were easy enough to identify.

Everybody in the room looked amazed. But it seemed that the most amazed of all was Wanda. Staring right at Mr. Pruitt, she stammered, "B-B-B-Bob?"

In a meek voice, Mr. Pruitt said, "W-W-Wanda. I can explain everything."

Wanda sprang to her feet and hurried away from the table.

Hmm . . . Wishbone thought. *I don't think Wanda's too happy about this turn of events.*

As Mr. Pruitt started to go after Wanda, he accidentally jerked the cord on his microphone. A loud pop sounded. It was followed by a small explosion of showering electrical sparks.

When Mr. Pruitt saw there was no damage done, he ran after Wanda. Most every head in the restaurant turned to watch, including Wishbone's.

"You know," Wishbone whispered to Joe, "this soap

opera is too good to miss. Keep some pizza warm for me. I'll be right back."

Wishbone jumped off Joe's lap and dashed after Mr. Pruitt, who was dashing after Wanda. Wanda pushed through the front door of the restaurant. A few steps later, Mr. Pruitt pushed through the door. Hanging right at Mr. Pruitt's heels, Wishbone was able to dart outside at the same time. It was a technique the dog had perfected through years of practice.

Wanda stood on the sidewalk in front of Pepper Pete's. As she fished through her purse, she muttered, "Oh, why can't I ever find a tissue when I need one?"

Mr. Pruitt walked up to her and said, "Wanda, I need to talk to you."

Wanda glanced at Mr. Pruitt. Her face showed a mixture of anger and deep hurt. Wishbone wasn't sure if she was going to give him an angry lecture, or burst into tears. It looked as if it could go either way.

Wishbone watched. *Yes, indeed,* he thought, *I have a feeling this is going to be the soap opera scene of the year.*

Wanda pointed an angry finger at Mr. Pruitt. "That was a very cruel thing to do, Bob Pruitt! The other night, when I came in here, you flirted with me while you pretended to be Lou Dublin. You even gave me your sunglasses and said you hoped to see me again sometime. And you were acting so . . . cool. So . . . rock-and-roll. So . . . Elvis-like. Well, of course I fell for you. And you *let* me. You never said a word—not a single word—about who you really were!"

I see she's going for the lecture, Wishbone thought.

Mr. Pruitt looked shamefully at his shoes. His physical appearance now seemed rather funny. Hanging down from his blond hair were Lou Dublin's bushy black sideburns. And Wishbone could see from his close-up view that Mr. Pruitt was wearing thick stage makeup. His appearance hardly seemed respectable for a teacher of middle-school English.

"Oh, Wanda," Mr. Pruitt said, "I never dreamed in a million years that you would be at that contest."

"Well, I was!" Wanda shot back.

"Yes, you were," Mr. Pruitt said with a nod. "And you looked so lovely sitting there. The moment I saw you that night, even though I was performing my act, I couldn't take my eyes off you."

Wanda's glare melted away for a moment. Then, as if it were a mask, she put it right back on. "Even so, you should have told me who you really were."

"I . . . I . . . was going to tell you," Mr. Pruitt said.

"When?" Wanda demanded. "After I had made a total fool of myself?"

"No, no, no," Mr. Pruitt insisted. "I was going to tell you that very night. But then . . . I decided not to. I was going to tell you the next morning—right after I told you that I wouldn't be able to take you to the poetry reading

117

we were planning to attend tonight. That's why I showed up on your doorstep with a bouquet of flowers. I didn't want you to be mad at me. But then . . . I don't know . . . I chickened out."

Wanda seemed to be fighting back tears. In a trembling voice, she said, "Well, of all things—Bob Pruitt, king of rock-and-roll! Who would ever have thought that? Certainly not stupid old me!"

Now she's going for the tears, I see, Wishbone thought.

Mr. Pruitt reached into his pocket and pulled out a handkerchief. He handed it to Wanda. Immediately, she used it to blow her nose.

"Wanda, it's like this," Mr. Pruitt explained. "About a month ago, I saw an ad for a talent contest here at Pepper Pete's. I had done some singing in college, and I thought it would be fun.

"Well, I've always been a big Elvis fan. So I figured, why not see how good an Elvis imitation I can do? I bought this costume and spent some time rehearsing. I found myself having a good time. I guess I got fairly good, because—what do you know—I won the contest!"

Wanda blew her nose again. Then she said, "You weren't bad at all. In fact, you were fantastic."

"But let me tell you something," Mr. Pruitt said. "The life of a rock-and-roll star is no picnic. I've been up to all hours the past few nights rehearsing. I was even late for school this morning. That has never happened to me before. And I sort of threw my shoulder out with all those wild arm movements."

Yeah, Wishbone thought, *sometimes I strain a paw when I've done too much heavy digging.*

After blowing her nose a third time, Wanda said, "But I don't understand something. Why didn't you tell me about your double life yesterday, when we were in my yard? I understand if you don't want a lot of people to know. But we were all alone at the time."

Well, almost all alone, Wishbone thought.

Mr. Pruitt released a nervous breath. "When I told you I wouldn't be able to take you to the poetry reading, you didn't seem to mind very much. In fact, I got the feeling you had something else you wanted to do.

"Then I caught a glimpse of those sunglasses Lou Dublin had given you. You were holding them at the time. At that moment, I realized that you liked Lou Dublin a lot better than you liked stuffy old Bob Pruitt. I was pretty upset about that at first. But then I got to thinking . . ."

Wanda finished the thought. ". . . that I would most likely show up tonight. Then you decided to let me fall for you as Lou Dublin."

"It doesn't make any sense," Mr. Pruitt said with a helpless shrug. "But I guess that's what I was thinking."

"Well, the truth is," Wanda confessed, "I was thinking Lou Dublin might be nice for a change."

"Sure," Mr. Pruitt said, looking down sadly. "I understand."

Wanda lifted Mr. Pruitt's chin very gently. "But that's not how I feel now. All you have to do is be yourself. And I guess I ought to be just myself, too. Look at me, wearing this crazy black outfit. The fact is, the real Wanda Gilmore likes the real Bob Pruitt a whole lot."

Mr. Pruitt showed a smile. "And the real Bob Pruitt likes the real Wanda Gilmore a whole lot."

Wanda and Mr. Pruitt looked at each other's outfits. At the same time, they both burst out laughing as if they were a couple of school kids.

Wishbone chuckled along, being careful not to be overheard.

119

"Oh, Bob, Bob, Bob," Wanda said, as she gave Mr. Pruitt a big hug.

"Oh, Wanda, Wanda, Wanda," Mr. Pruitt said, as he hugged her back.

"Ah, this is just great," Wishbone said. "The most romantic scene I've witnessed in a long time. Now, why don't the three of us go back inside? We can laugh this whole silly thing off by chowing down another couple of pizza pies. The treat's on me."

Wanda and Mr. Pruitt seemed to be much too busy hugging to hear the dog's suggestion.

So the mystery is finally explained! At least the one concerning Mr. Pruitt and Lou Dublin.

Now, maybe we can hightail it back to London and sneak a peek at that letter. We may finally get an explanation about that Jekyll-and-Hyde mystery.

Uh . . . wait a second. Are we *sure* we really want that explanation?

CHAPTER FOURTEEN

Outside Utterson's house, the wind howled and shrieked, as if the very air itself were filled with demons.

Utterson sat on the red-leather chair in his study, alone and thoughtful. A cheery fire crackled in the fireplace, but the lawyer felt little of its warmth. Utterson knew that he held a chilling secret. He was holding the letter from Henry Jekyll that he had discovered in the doctor's laboratory only an hour ago.

The envelope was still sealed. Utterson was not yet certain he wished to read the letter. He knew it would reveal the very information that was so disturbing it had caused Hastie Lanyon, the healthiest of men, to die from shock.

Indeed, Utterson thought, *curiosity not only killed the cat, but it killed Hastie Lanyon, as well. There's no telling what it shall do to me. However, Henry Jekyll was my friend and client. I suppose I have a duty to see to his wishes until the bitter end, no matter what the risk may be.*

With no further delay, Utterson broke the envelope's several wax seals. He reached in and pulled out the letter, which was written on quite a few sheets of paper.

121

By the glow of the nearby gas lamp, Utterson began to read:

MY dear Gabriel,

Early in my life, I discovered that I was basically a very good man. I valued hard work, sought the respect of those around me, and felt a deep devotion to my church. On this foundation, I set out to build for myself a most perfect and honorable life.

Yet, during my college days, I discovered another side to my personality—perhaps an evil one. I found myself drawn to life's dangerous pleasures. By this I mean liquor, parties, gambling, luxury, and so forth. For a while, I let myself roam a bit among these playgrounds of pleasure.

Nevertheless, I had decided to live a wholesome life. Upon my graduation from college, I shut out the negative pleasures entirely. I devoted every ounce of my energy to serving my fellowman through my medical practice. For a time, I was quite happy. After a number of years, however, I felt a desire once again to sample those pleasures that I had vowed never to try again.

I realized, of course, that a life of continuous vice could not mix with a life of honor. And so perfect did I try to be that I allowed myself not a single one of those old pleasures.

Yet, this other side of my personality continued to have a strong pull on me. With some humor, I thought to myself that it would be convenient if a person could split himself into two entirely different people. After all, does not every person have aspects of both good and evil?

Then I began to wonder if such a miracle might actually be scientifically possible.

My research methods were always rather unusual. In my laboratory, I had created many medicines that were previously unknown by those in the medical community. I had come to understand that the human body is really just a complex collection of chemicals. If treated properly with other chemicals, the human body was capable of undergoing amazing changes. Often, those were for the better, but sometimes for the worse.

For a period of several years, I worked hard on my ground-breaking new idea. I searched for a chemical mixture that might allow a human being to actually divide itself into two separate people.

I realize that such a task sounds wildly unbelievable. However, after much trial and error, I created a potion that I believed would bring about just such an incredible change.

I will not reveal to you, or anyone, the exact recipe of this potion. First, this was an experiment too dreadful ever to be attempted again. Second, my discoveries were incomplete. It is enough to say that the day finally came for me to sample the potion.

Utterson felt his muzzle open slowly with wonder.

As he stroked a whisker, he continued to read. The next section of the letter interested the lawyer even more—so much more that he saw it not as words on the page, but as a living scene in his mind.

Utterson imagined Henry Jekyll standing alone in his laboratory. The doctor was preparing to take his first drink of his experimental potion. . . .

With careful hands, Dr. Jekyll picked up a small bottle containing a blood-red liquid. After uncorking the bottle, he poured its contents into a measuring glass. Next, he unfolded a square of paper that contained a powdery pile of tiny white crystals. He poured the crystals into the glass and then stirred it into the red liquid with a glass rod.

Dr. Jekyll stepped back. He stared intently at the glass. As the powder melted, the liquid began to hiss, fizz, and bubble rapidly. Gradually, the blood-red liquid darkened to a deep purple. Soon the bubbling eased away. The purple liquid, as if by magic, faded into a shade of pale green.

His hand now trembling, Jekyll placed his fingers around the glass. He lifted the glass to the level of his mouth.

The doctor hesitated. He knew if his calculations were wrong, the potion could cause his instant death . . . or perhaps something even worse. Jekyll thought briefly of tossing the liquid down the sink, and yet . . . he could not.

Jekyll touched the glass to his lips. Tilting back his head, he poured the liquid into his mouth. He swallowed every last drop in a single gulp. The potion tasted much like water, with perhaps a faint trace of peppermint. It was rather pleasant and harmless. He set down the empty glass. He felt no different from the way he had felt ten seconds before.

A few moments passed, with no result. The doctor laughed. He realized this potion he had worked on for so long might have no effect.

The next second, the doctor's hand flew out, knocking the glass to the ground. The glass shattered. A violent pain was shooting through every inch of the doctor's

body. It felt as if a dozen strong hands were tearing him to shreds, ripping the muscles and tendons beneath his flesh. Jekyll doubled over and staggered around the room, crashing into the walls and furniture.

A short time later, as quickly as the pain came, it disappeared. The doctor felt as fine as he had before he drank the potion—no, actually better. Yes—much, much better. At once he felt younger, lighter, happier. A sweet tingling sensation swept through his body. Dr. Jekyll stretched his arms high above his head, feeling as if he had just been released from the tight quarters of a prison cell and had been let out into the light.

The doctor's heart skipped a beat as he caught a glimpse of his hand. It was much changed. It seemed smaller but muscular. There were growths of hair upon the knuckles.

Jekyll wanted to take a look at himself, but there was no mirror in the laboratory. It was the dead of night, and he knew there was no risk of running into one of his servants. He raced from his laboratory across the courtyard. He entered his house and ran right for the privacy of his bedroom. There he turned his face upon a mirror.

"My God! What have I done?" Jekyll gasped.

The creature staring back at him was nothing like his former self. He was shorter, hairier, stronger, uglier. His physical movements were quick and jerky. His body was a little stooped over. The teeth were rotten and crooked.

In addition, everything about him in some way seemed a bit . . . monstrous. Deep inside, the doctor felt a sense of incredible disgust. Yet, to the doctor's surprise, a devilish smile crossed the creature's lips. Jekyll realized it wasn't himself smiling—but an entirely different person!

The creature hurried back to his laboratory. There he mixed up another glass of the potion. He gulped it, then thrashed around with more physical agony. When the pain disappeared, the creature glanced at his hand, which had gone back to its normal, human-like appearance. The creature realized that he had changed back into Henry Jekyll.

With tremendous joy, Jekyll's heart seemed to soar through the ceiling of the laboratory. He realized his experiment had been a complete success!

Utterson set the letter aside.

He felt dizzy, as if he had been chasing his tail around and around for hours on end. The whole idea of the changeover was impossible, yet he knew it was true. He realized that Dr. Jekyll and Mr. Hyde were the exact same person. At the same time, though, they were two separate persons. Twins that were complete opposites. Two sides of the same coin.

Utterson continued to read the letter:

I tested the potion several more times. Each time it worked incredibly well. I realized my dream had come true. I could follow both sides of my personality by leading lives as two entirely different persons.

I named the creature "Edward Hyde," and I set about preparing his life. I told all my servants that Mr. Hyde would be making occasional visits to my house and laboratory. He was to have the complete run of those places, even if I was not home.

Then I drew up the will, the one you objected to so strongly. I did this because I knew there was always a

127

slight chance something would go wrong with the potion, preventing Hyde from turning back to Jekyll. While in the body of Hyde, I rented the rooms in Soho and had them decorated to Hyde's liking.

Finally, I began to enjoy the fruits of my labor. Every so often, perhaps once or twice a month, I would drink the potion in my laboratory and change myself into Hyde. Then I'd leave the laboratory and do whatever I pleased. I'd go to my Soho rooms or somewhere out in the city. Much like a schoolboy after class, I dove right into a life of extreme pleasure. I enjoyed wild parties, endless bottles of wine, and the most delicious of meals. I confess, I found these experiences to be thrilling!

When I had had enough, temporarily, of my reckless self, I returned to the laboratory and drank myself back into the person of Jekyll. The changeovers, I might add, gradually turned speedier and much less painful.

The truly wonderful part of the arrangement was this: The two separate lives did not interfere with each other the least bit. Jekyll didn't really care what Hyde did, and Hyde certainly didn't care one bit about Jekyll. I was allowed to explore both sides of my personality fully and freely.

Occasionally, Hyde got himself into trouble. You see, the man had no conscience, no sense of right and wrong. This led him from doing minor misdeeds to committing acts of extreme evil.

He began to enjoy hurting others. That is why Hyde once trampled a young girl who accidentally bumped into him. On a few occasions he struck someone who said or did something not to his liking.

Hyde discovered, however, that he could smooth

these situations over by writing out a check from Jekyll's checkbook. Hyde's handwriting was a little clumsy, but it was similar enough to Jekyll's to satisfy the bank employees.

For a number of months, all went well. I was the happiest of men. Then Hyde seemed to grow wilder and wilder. He had absolutely no control of himself.

The situation reached a crisis stage when Hyde beat Sir Danvers Carew to death with that cane you had once given to me. Why did he do this? For no other reason than the twisted fact that he wanted to. I suppose it was a way for him to express his feeling of being totally free.

That night, even while I was still in Hyde's body, I realized it was time to end this dangerous game. This was partly because the police would be after Hyde. Mostly, though, I had no stomach for such wickedness anymore.

The Jekyll in me forced Hyde to write that note I gave to you—the one that said Hyde would no longer bother Jekyll. I suppose I did this as a sort of promise that Hyde would never return. I was still hesitant to change the will, however; I was concerned that something unexpected might happen.

I drank the potion no more. I threw myself into my medical practice with more energy than ever. I worked to find cures for the most awful diseases. I began to see many patients, even if they could not afford my fees. I went to church often. I was doing whatever I could to make myself the very perfect picture of decency.

Then the dream turned into a nightmare.

Utterson gave his side a nervous scratch with his back paw. He knew something unsettling was coming up.

Utterson read on, his fur bristling. Again he began to see the words as a living scene.

He pictured Henry Jekyll sitting most peacefully on a park bench. . . .

Jekyll looked around at the pleasant surroundings. Snow was melting on the ground, and people were out strolling. Somewhere a bird chirped, eager for the healing warmth of spring.

Suddenly, Jekyll felt a slight faintness in his head. There was also a vague tensing of his muscles. It was nothing severe. He figured it might have been something from his lunch that did not agree with him.

Ignoring the irritation, the doctor pulled a small book from his pocket and opened it. His eyes turned to the page. Then his eyes fell on the two hands holding the book.

They were the hands of Edward Hyde!

The doctor stared at the hands in disbelief. Fearfully, he felt his coat. It was now several sizes too large. The same was true of his hat, trousers, shirt, and shoes. The doctor reached up, and he touched wild hair and long, bristling sideburns.

With a rapidly pounding heart, Jekyll realized that he was no longer himself. He had changed into Hyde *without drinking the potion!* All of a sudden! Against his will!

Hyde looked around in a state of panic. He knew every policeman in the city was on the lookout for him. What's more, many citizens knew of his physical appearance from the pictures they had seen in the newspapers. No doubt they would be eager to turn him in to the authorities so they could collect the thousand-pound reward offered for his capture.

Hyde's first thought was to rush back to the laboratory and change over to Jekyll. Immediately. But then he realized that would not be possible. The entrances to Jekyll's house and his laboratory were under constant watch by the police.

Hyde felt trapped, angry, afraid, like a hunted beast. He rubbed his misshapen head, desperately trying to think of a means of turning back into Jekyll. That was the only way to escape.

He thought of Jekyll's old friend, Hastie Lanyon. Perhaps he could help. Hyde ripped pen and paper from his oversized coat and began to scrawl a note to Lanyon.

Once more, Utterson set down the letter. The fur along his back was standing straight up. He knew what had happened next. Lanyon fetched the ingredients for the potion. Hyde showed up at his house. Then Lanyon witnessed Hyde changing back into Jekyll—right before his very eyes!

No wonder poor Hastie suffered such a shock, Utterson thought with a whisker twitch. *I'm not sure I could have survived such a nightmarish scene myself. The act of reading about it is difficult enough.*

Utterson returned his eyes to the letter. . . .

I know I was responsible for Lanyon's death. This knowledge has caused me great pain. From the day after

that horrid event, I continued to change into Hyde without the benefit of the potion. It always happened against my wishes. It generally happened once or twice a day. As a result, I never left the shelter of my property. This is the state I was in when you saw me that time staring out my window from the street below.

Both of my lives became filled with terror. Hyde was terrified of hanging on the gallows; Jekyll was terrified of being Hyde. Each time I turned to Hyde, the Jekyll in me struggled, forcing Hyde to drink the potion that changed him back to Jekyll.

The changeover began to require stronger doses of the potion. This is because Hyde was becoming stronger than Jekyll. The more Jekyll struggled to hold off Hyde from appearing, the more powerful Hyde grew when he came into being.

Soon the changes came more often. I seldom left the lab, knowing Jekyll might change into Hyde at any moment. The powders began to run low so I ordered more of them. To my horror, the new supply didn't work. I sent Poole to every druggist in the city. I hoped he would find a mixture that was more pure.

But then I discovered that in my original mixture, one of the powders contained a slight impurity—one that was necessary in order for the potion to work. Unfortunately, that exact impurity could never again be duplicated. I realized when I ran out of my original supply that Mr. Hyde would never again be able to change back to Dr. Jekyll.

This evening, as I write this letter, I have no more of the original powders. The next time I change into Hyde, Henry Jekyll will be gone forever. This is fine by Mr. Hyde, but it is not acceptable to me. I prefer death.

A short while ago I wrote out my new will. I am leaving

everything to You, dear Gabriel. Your deep concern for my welfare throughout this HORrid eXperIENce has touCHed mE greatLY.

At thIS verY mOMent, I FEEL Mr. HYde enTERING mE. I mUST BRINg this storY to a close. I LET You DECIdE WHAT TO DO with it.

Yes, I mUST SEt down MY PEN aND CarRY OUT MY FINAL ACt at oNce. When MR. HYDE BREAKS THROUGH, HE WILL DO EVERYthing in hiS POWER TO PREVENT mY esCApe frOM HIS CLUTCHES. I CAN ONLY PRAY THAT I triUMPH.

YOuR MOST HUmBLE FRiEND,
HENRY JEKYLL.

On the signature, the handwriting began to change. Utterson felt his tail shiver with icy fear. He realized that even as Henry Jekyll was finishing the letter, Mr. Hyde was invading the doctor's body and mind.

Utterson knew enough to imagine what the final events would be like. . . .

Jekyll set down his pen and he quickly drank the poison. Very soon after, he changed into Hyde for the last time. As the poison did its deadly work, Utterson and Poole tried to get into the lab.

There must have been a tiny bit of Jekyll remaining inside of Hyde, and he refused to let the two men in. He probably feared they would send for a doctor and manage to save Hyde. The death must have happened as Poole was attacking the door with the axe. Indeed, Jekyll had triumphed in the end. With that final act, Jekyll's goodness had managed to overpower Hyde's evil.

Utterson sat quietly for a long while. He listened to the wild wind outside.

With whom should I share this story? Utterson thought, as he stroked a whisker. *Friends? Scientists? The newspapers? No. Oh, no. This is a secret that should never be passed on. Like Lanyon, the world might not survive the shock. I have no doubt that if the doctor's experiment were made public, soon others would attempt it, and then . . .*

Utterson stuck the letter in his mouth and jumped down from the leather chair. He trotted over to the fireplace, turned his muzzle, then flung every sheet of the letter into the dancing flames.

The lawyer lay on his belly beside the fire, finally feeling some of its comforting warmth.

"Is there a lesson to be learned from all of this?" Utterson wondered out loud to himself. "If so, perhaps it is this: If a person tries too hard to be perfect in every way, as Henry Jekyll did, something is bound to backfire sooner or later—with or without a chemical potion. After all, we are only human. We do make mistakes."

Utterson licked a paw, developing his theory further.

"We should follow the golden rule, and try never to harm our fellowman. That's obvious enough. But, say, if a person desires a sausage now and then, he should allow himself to have a sausage now and then.

"I believe that I have stumbled onto a small bit of wisdom. Tomorrow morning I intend to go straight to Alexander's Butcher Shop. There I shall purchase a chain of those delectable-looking sausages I have so often admired."

Utterson licked his chops, almost tasting the tempting treat on his tongue.

"No—wait. Tomorrow is Sunday. The butcher shop will be closed. I'll purchase the sausage on Monday. Ah, yes, tomorrow I shall be taking my weekly Sunday stroll with my dear cousin Enfield. Shall I tell him anything of the terrible secret I have learned tonight? He is most curious about the affair. No—perish the thought. I shall never reveal to him or anyone else the truth about the very strange case of Dr. Jekyll and Mr. Hyde."

Gabriel John Utterson watched the last of the letter burn and curl into a collection of ashes.

Hmm . . . So were Dr. Jekyll and Mr. Hyde really the same person? A strange case, indeed . . .

CHAPTER FIFTEEN

The following morning, the school bell rang. The clock on the wall of Mr. Pruitt's classroom showed exactly 9:30.

Wishbone knew this because he was watching through the classroom window. He was perched on the bag of lawn fertilizer. All the students were in their seats, leafing frantically through the pages of their poetry textbooks.

Wishbone knew any minute now the kids would be taking their dreaded poetry test. The dog felt he should be around to lend his friends emotional support.

I hope Joe, Sam, and David do okay, Wishbone thought. *I did my very best coaching them. And I hope they realize I was only kidding about the William Steakespeare thing. It wouldn't look too good if one of them actually wrote down that name as an answer!*

Wishbone saw Joe brush his hair off his forehead several times. It was something that he did when he was especially worried.

The classroom door swung open, and Mr. Pruitt made his entrance. This morning he looked exactly like, well, the regular Mr. Pruitt. His clothes were perfectly neat, his hair was nicely combed, and he wore a pleasant expression on his face. On top of that, the man seemed very happy. He was whistling a classical-music melody that Wishbone recognized.

Upon reaching his desk, Mr. Pruitt set down his briefcase and announced cheerfully, "Good morning, everybody!"

"Good morning," the students said all together. To Wishbone's ear, none of them sounded too enthusiastic. In fact, there was a groaning tone to most of their voices. Wishbone knew this was because of the test that was lying in wait inside Mr. Pruitt's briefcase.

"Sounds like everyone is ready for today's examination," Mr. Pruitt said with a sly smile. "Good. I am, too."

A nervous murmur moved through the room.

Mr. Pruitt walked around to the front of his desk and leaned against it. "First, I would like to say something," he said. He folded his arms on his chest in a teacherly fashion. "Last night, I saw three of my students at a certain pizza parlor here in town."

Joe, Sam, and David exchanged worried looks.

Uh-oh, Wishbone thought, watching every move. *I have a feeling Mr. Pruitt is going to lecture them about going out on a school night. And not just any school night. The eve of an important poetry test.*

"These three students," Mr. Pruitt continued, "had their poetry textbooks with them. They were reading poetry aloud to one another—right there at their table, as they ate their pizza. They were reading the poems rather well, I might add. And their dedication to their studies touched me very deeply. It gave me an idea for this morning's test."

Oh, great, Wishbone thought. *Their dedication inspired him to make the test even more difficult.*

"This morning's test," Mr. Pruitt announced with pride, "is going to be a *taste* test. Today we will examine the beauty and perfection and—yes—the artistry of . . . pizza. That's right. Even though it's just the morning, I have ordered pizza for everybody. Nothing wrong with bending the lunch schedule now and then. The pizza should be here in just a few minutes."

Sounds of astonishment went around the whole classroom. Soon those sounds turned into laughter, signs of relief, and even some scattered applause.

Mr. Pruitt gave a polite bow of his head. Then his expression changed as he noticed something outside the window.

Oh, no! Wishbone thought fearfully. *He sees me! I'm not supposed to be here. The school has a very clearcut 'no dogs' policy. I hope I don't get sent to the principal's office!*

Mr. Pruitt gave the dog a friendly wink. The funny thing was, it looked a lot like a wink Wishbone had seen Lou Dublin give.

"Dig, dig, dig," Wishbone called out. His front paws tore through the dirt in one of Wanda's flower beds. Unfortunately, Mr. Pruitt had not invited the dog into the classroom to share in the pizza party. But the thought of pizza made Wishbone so hungry that he had dashed straight for Wanda's yard. If all went well, he would soon have a nice tough bone to snack on.

As he dug, Wishbone noticed the leaves were falling more rapidly, and the air was turning chillier. This reminded the dog that Halloween was very close, indeed. Soon the neighborhood would be crawling with ghosts and monsters and witches. . . .

Wishbone's ears picked up the sound of approaching footsteps. Scary footsteps. Wanda's footsteps!

Wishbone stopped digging, feeling a wave of panic wash over him. Then he relaxed. He remembered that the *new* Wanda didn't mind him digging in her flower garden. At least she didn't seem to mind the other day.

Just keep on digging, Wishbone thought, as his paws went back to work. *There is nothing to worry about.*

"Wishbone!" Wanda yelled, as she came stomping over. "This is a disaster! You are ruining this flower bed!"

On second thought, Wishbone realized as his paws stopped doing their work, *maybe there is something to worry about, after all.*

Wishbone turned around. Wanda crouched down and began to wag an angry finger in the dog's face. "Now, listen to me, you bad dog! You devil of a dirt-digger! You outlaw flower-killer! I will not have you destroying . . ."

Wishbone had heard this lecture many times before, and he didn't need to hear it again. He raced away as fast

as his four legs would carry him. Behind him, the dog could hear Wanda continuing with the lecture at high volume.

Now, that's *the Wanda Gilmore I used to know!* Wishbone thought as he ran. *And I guess I'm glad Wanda's back to her regular self—even if that means I get yelled at sometimes. To be honest, I was a little uncomfortable with her being so different. Because, you know, people should be . . . well . . . themselves. Whatever that happens to be.*

While we're on the subject, I'm sure glad Mr. Pruitt is back to his regular self. And, personally, I hope I'm never anything but the handsome, intelligent, wonderful dog I am right now!

About Robert Louis Stevenson

Robert Louis Balfour Stevenson was born on November 13, 1850, in Edinburgh, Scotland, to a family of lighthouse engineers. As an only child, he was expected to follow in his family's footsteps. But Stevenson had no interest in building lighthouses. Instead, he decided to go into law and attended Edinburgh University to study for a law degree. While there, he eventually discovered his real passion: writing.

Stevenson went on to write a number of novels, short stories, poems, essays, and plays. His first critical and popular success was *Treasure Island*, which began when he created a game to amuse his young stepson, Lloyd. His other major works include *A Child's Garden of Verses*, *Kidnapped*, *The Master of Ballantraw*, and the unfinished novel *Weir of Hermiston*.

Stevenson was troubled by breathing ailments all of his life. His poor physical health led him to travel widely, mostly in search of warm, dry climates. Fortunately, this suited his love of adventure, as well. His journeys inspired the plots of many of his novels and short stories.

In 1889, Stevenson and his family sailed from Scotland to Samoa, an island in the South Pacific Ocean, and they settled there. Stevenson died on the island in 1894.

Engraved upon his tombstone in Samoa are some lines from one of his poems:

> *Here he lies where he longed to be;*
> *Home is the sailor, home from sea,*
> *And the hunter home from the hill.*

About *Strange Case of Dr. Jekyll and Mr. Hyde*

One night in 1885, Robert Louis Stevenson was having a bad dream. Hearing him crying out in his sleep, his wife, Fanny, woke him up. "Why did you awaken me?" he asked her. "I was dreaming a fine bogey-tale."

The next morning, Stevenson began to work feverishly on a new story. Lying in bed and warning his family not to bother him for any reason, he wrote almost continuously for the next three days.

At the end of that time, Stevenson sat his family down and read to them the story of the clean-living Dr. Jekyll and the evil Mr. Hyde. As soon as he was finished, however, Fanny began to criticize it. She told her husband that he had written a weak horror story when it could have been a real masterpiece.

Angry at her criticism but still taking it seriously, Stevenson burned the entire manuscript. He then began all over again, and wrote furiously for another three days. This time, both Fanny and Stevenson were pleased by the results. He had created a believable and complex tale of tragedy.

Published in 1886, *Strange Case of Dr. Jekyll and Mr. Hyde* went on to become an instant success in both England and America. It remains popular to this day, and the phrase "Jekyll and Hyde" is now a common expression used to describe a person who seems to be split into two separate personalities.

About Nancy Butcher

Nancy Butcher does not have two personalities—at least not that she knows of, anyway. But years ago, when she worked as a book editor, she began to feel that there was another part of her struggling to be unleashed. It was Nancy Butcher the writer, and that part of her completely took over in 1992. Nancy Butcher the editor was never to be heard from again.

Since 1992, Nancy has published thirteen children's books, including four Ghostwriter mysteries (*Daycamp Nightmare, Disaster on Wheels, Creepy Sleepaway,* and *Caught in the Net*). She's also written a mystery radioplay for youngsters, a number of short stories for the Bepuzzled/Spider Tales series, and some titles for adults, too.

Born in Tokyo, Japan, Nancy also lived in Ohio, Chicago, California, and New York City before settling down in Saratoga Springs, New York. She lives in an old, bat-filled house—built about ten years before Stevenson wrote *Strange Case of Dr. Jekyll and Mr. Hyde*—with her husband, Philip Reynolds; their son, Christopher; and their three cats, Fanny, Ming, and Mouse.

In her spare time, Nancy watches lots of movies, plays the piano, and enjoys the outdoors. She also loves reading; nineteenth-century novels and mysteries (of any century!) are among her favorites.